WOLVERHAMPTON PUBLIC LIBRARIES
WITHDRAWN FROM CIRCULATION AND SOLD
45P RECEIVED BY NS

07278 522 214 535 C4

THE POPPY FIELD

Recent Titles by Christine Marion Fraser from Severn House

ULLIN MACBETH
WILD IS THE DAY
THE POPPY FIELD

THE POPPY FIELD

Christine Marion Fraser and Frank Ian Galloway

This first world edition published in Great Britain 1997 by
SEVERN HOUSE PUBLISHERS LTD of
9–15 High Street, Sutton, Surrey SM1 1DF.
First published in the U.S.A. 1997 by
SEVERN HOUSE PUBLISHERS INC., of
595 Madison Avenue, New York, NY 10022.

Copyright © 1997 by Christine Marion Fraser and Frank Ian Galloway.

All rights reserved.
The moral right of the author has been asserted.

British Library Cataloguing in Publication Data

Fraser, Christine Marion
    The poppy field
    1.   Domestic fiction
    I   Title
    II   Galloway, Frank Ian
    823.9'14 [F]

    ISBN 0-7278-5222-1

All situations in this publication are fictitious and
any resemblance to living persons is purely coincidental.

Typeset by Palimpsest Book Production Limited,
Polmont, Stirlingshire, Scotland.
Printed and bound in Great Britain by
Hartnolls Ltd, Bodmin, Cornwall.

*From Frank
To Millie, My Little Songbird.*

Chapter One

The little chameleon slowly climbed up the stone wall that Velana was sitting on, its eyes darting back and forth with peripheral vision as, sensing the girl's presence, it hesitated for a moment before slowly moving off to disappear among the bushes.

A little smile touched Velana's lips as she wondered if perhaps its mate was waiting for it somewhere among the thick sun-warmed undergrowth beneath the wall.

She, too, was waiting for someone, someone very special and her heart missed a beat as the well-loved voice of her sweetheart, Jose, came echoing down to her from the top of the hill, calling her name in that warm, deep, wonderful voice of his. She held her breath and felt the blood tingling in her veins as he came bounding down the hill towards her.

She had known Jose all her young life. She was sixteen and he was seventeen. They lived in neighbouring farms, near the small town of Olhão in southern Portugal. She had grown up with him and his two brothers, Miguel and Pedro. All of them had gone to school and church together and now that they were old enough they helped with the work of growing and harvesting citrus fruits on their parents' farm.

Velana had loved Jose for as long as she could remember. As children they had played in the stalactite caverns and ravines among the hills of the surrounding countryside, pretending that he was a prince and she his princess in make-believe games; in the summer they had bathed and swum in the numerous deep pools in the underground caverns and had vowed that they would love one another forever.

But this was a different kind of love. This was a love burning deep inside her, one that enveloped every part of her being. As she watched his tall, strong figure coming nearer she saw his flashing dark eyes crinkling into a smile that lit the handsome contours of his face.

"Velana, you look wonderful," he greeted her huskily, stretching out his arms to her. Suddenly shy of one another, they embraced and kissed, very aware of the precious thing that had grown so strong between them.

"Let's go," he said, "let's go to our secret place."

He gazed at her and wondered afresh at her beauty, this tall, blonde blue-eyed, slender girl with her golden tan and the bubbly personality that had never ceased to fascinate him, even as a child.

Now she had blossomed into an enchanting young woman and he felt nervous and proud and excited all at the same time whenever he was near her.

Hand in hand they ran up the dusty road and across the poppy field where the air was heady with the scent of the sun-drenched flowers. Tiny moths flitted and danced in the fragrant air, colourful butterflies balanced themselves like little ballerinas on the spears of rosemary, and Velana felt giddy with the sweetness and wonder of the world that surrounded her.

She held Jose's hand tightly, feeling that she never wanted to let it go and turning to him she said quietly, "Can we go for a swim before we go home?"

Her voice was breathless and strange and he gazed at her, something in his eyes that made her heart beat swiftly in her breast.

Wordlessly he nodded and they walked on, their steps quickening as if they couldn't wait to get to the 'secret' place they had known since childhood.

At the edge of the field the ground fell away into a deep ravine and a little winding path led them down into the cool stalactite caverns. This was 'their' place; together they had swam and laughed in the subterranean caves, had confided their childish hopes and dreams to one another, listing all the things they would like to do when they grew up.

The days of their young adulthood were with them now, childish things were forgotten. Jose stripped off his shirt, Velana removed only her shoes; the dress she was wearing was so thin it would be no deterrent to her in the water. They plunged together into the pool, holding hands once more as they went down into the cool, dark, silken depths, surfacing a few minutes later to swim in circles, splashing one another, diving and kissing under water among the dancing air bubbles.

When they had exhausted themselves they lay on their backs and floated, the water cradling and soothing them. Silence was all around them. They were as acutely aware of it as they were of each other and a powerful stillness came over them. It was as if the world had stopped turning and they were caught in the middle of timeless moments that they knew they would remember in days and years to come.

Then everything began to move and change. The sandstone walls and arches of the cavern became flooded with luminosity, making stones and rocks look like gold, and green embers scattered across the sandy floor. The light played on the sand, making it look like sparkling crystals, a white diffusion of shining lines and beams shone and danced into every nook and cranny till the whole cave became illuminated with myriad dancing reflections.

"Jose!" gasped Velana. "What's happening?"

Without waiting for his answer she quickly scrambled out of the water to stare around her in awe while droplets of water fell from her naked limbs and dress and cascaded around her like sparkling stars.

"It's all right," laughed Jose, putting an arm round her shoulders. "It's the phosphorescence in the water reflecting the low sun rays in the caverns. It only happens when conditions are just right and it might be years before it happens again."

Velana looked at him and in her highly emotional state she thought he looked like a young god, with the strong profile of his face etched against the sun's golden beams. Gently she traced the lines of his cheek with one tremulous finger.

He gazed down at her upturned face; his mouth met hers, she could feel his heart beating against her breasts. They looked at each other for a long, long time then they gathered up their clothes and shoes and went outside.

Low-slung on the cobalt horizon, the sun was a ball of fire, the scent of the poppy field drifted enticingly on the breath of evening, like a heady wine that drowned the senses of the two young people as they stood on the ridge, drinking in every sight, sound, and smell.

"Come on." There was an urgency in Jose's voice as he led Velana towards the poppy field. Just before they reached it she stumbled. He lifted her up in his muscular brown arms and carried her the rest of the way.

Gently he lowered her down into a bed of warm, fragrant wild flowers and touched her lips with his. The damp, flimsy material of her dress clung to every curve of her young body. Slowly he undid the buttons, his breath catching in his throat when he beheld the creamy whiteness of her breasts, the tempting curves of her thighs.

His lovely Velana, there was no one in the world like her, no one . . .

Her arms came up to bring his head down, their mouths met and merged; the night and the perfume of Portugal embraced them like a soft blanket, and they knew only that and the wonder they discovered in each other as the sun slowly dipped beneath the horizon, brushing the fields and the valleys with a golden, glowing light.

The pink afterglow of sunset allowed them to see where they were going when eventually they made their way homeward. Velana glanced back at the little dip in the field where she and Jose had made love for the very first time. Deep purple shadows filled all the scented hollows but she would always know which one was hers – hers and Jose's. It belonged to them for all time, no one would ever take away the magic of this night, this hour, these moments with her hand held tight and warm in his.

As if sensing her thoughts he pulled her closer. She felt safe and warm and wanted, yet – somehow a tiny bit sad. The days of her childhood were behind her now. Never again would she run in innocent delight with Jose through the waving grasses of the poppy field. That part of her life was over, tonight she had grown up, there was no turning back now.

Jose's grip on her hand tightened. Gently he kissed her on the lips. "Don't be sad, my dearest love," he said quietly. "Tonight our love for one another has been fulfilled. I'll remember this night for the rest of my life and so, I hope, will you." She didn't look back as she walked homewards with Jose through the ever-darkening countryside.

Velana's mother, Theresa Domingo, kept glancing out of the farmhouse window as she prepared the evening meal. The sun had set into the distant horizon, darkness was falling and she was becoming a bit concerned about her daughter, who never usually stayed out as late as this. She had choir practice tonight and had promised she would be home early.

Theresa caught sight of her reflection in the little mirror above the table. She was still quite attractive, she thought, even for her thirty-eight years. There were a few grey hairs at her temples, little laughter lines at the corner of her dark brown eyes, and she had grown a bit heavier round the hips in recent years, but all things considered she was still a fine-looking woman.

She glanced at her, husband, Mario, who was sitting in the corner of the room working away at his favourite hobby, making miniature 'icons'. A strange little smile flickered over her features as she observed him. Such an aura of peace about him, the way his hands moved as he worked, lovingly carving little frames and fashioning colourful pictures into works of art which he usually donated to church funds or gave away to friends.

He had always enjoyed working with his hands but of late she had noticed a trembling in them which he didn't seem able to control. He hadn't said anything to anyone of course, Mario never liked to make a fuss about himself but Theresa vowed to herself that she would try and persuade him to see the local doctor as soon as she could.

"Velana should be home by now," Mario said with a frown as he got up to brush his wood shavings from the tiled floor. "She shouldn't stay out as late as this, she knows when she ought to be in."

At that moment the door opened and Velana came in, laden down with two wooden buckets of water from the well outside in the yard.

"Hallo Mamma, hallo Papa," she greeted her parents somewhat breathlessly, "I'm sorry I'm late, I went for a walk with Jose and – and we forgot the time."

Theresa saw the radiant look on her daughter's face and knew that she was a woman now. A sense of poignancy touched Theresa's heart. She had always tried to give her daughter good and honest advice but sometimes that could so very easily be forgotten when youth and passion coursed free and strong in the blood . . .

"Come on, you've kept us all waiting for dinner," Theresa said a trifle abruptly. She took one of the buckets from her daughter's hand and set it down. "We'll have to get through the meal quickly," she continued, "Father Silvas wants you all to be early for choir practice as there's to be a committee meeting afterwards."

"All right, Mamma," answered Velana as she flitted about, setting the dinner places, humming to herself as she did so, performing little dance steps in time to the rhythm of her own voice.

Smiling a little, Mario took his place at the table. He loved to see his daughter happy and to hear her singing. She had a voice like an angel, high and sweet with a ring to it that often sent shivers through him, so profoundly could she move him.

The womenfolk sat down, Mario bowed his head and said grace. Velana looked at him with love in her eyes. He had taught her so much. Everything she knew about farming and fruit growing, plants and wild animals and birds, she had learned from him. His knowledge had been handed down through generations. Under his guidance she had become adept at making the local brew, medronho, from the arbutus plant, and she had also become good at distilling heather, lavender, and rosemary, for cough mixtures and medicines and much, much more.

He was respected and renowned in the area for his experience in many things and Velana always felt proud of him when people came to the farm to ask his advice on some problem or other.

The soup course was over, Velana removed the empty plates and Theresa carried the hot dish of sardines, potatoes, and lemon, from the ancient hearth in the centre of the room, and placed it on the table.

"Ah, Mamma Theresa." Mario looked at his wife and smiled. "This smells wonderful. Thanks to Velana keeping us waiting, my appetite tonight is huge." He poured the wine, his hand, thankfully, remaining steady. Raising his glass he clicked it with his forefinger. The ring of the crystal made a very satisfying sound. "To the two most wonderful women in my life," he said quietly. "I have been truly blessed with your love."

Theresa looked at Velana and a smile touched her lips; she looked at her husband and a tear pricked the corner of her eyelid. "To all of us," she said, "good health and happiness. Nothing is more important than that." They chinked their glasses together, the tinkling sounds chimed through the room. After that, little more was said till the meal was finished.

Chapter Two

Farmer Miguel Rodrigas senior, his wife Maria, and their three sons, Miguel junior, Jose, and Pedro, were the first to arrive at the church hall. Maria, who was very devout and religious, was self-appointed caretaker of the building. She was a good organiser and was keen to be in the forefront of the preparations for the coming celebrations of the feast of 'St Joseph the Worker'. She was anxious for her husband and sons to be involved in the event, even to the point of nagging them into doing something worthwhile.

Farmer Rodrigas was an easy-going type of man with a portly figure and a large walrus moustache. He could be outspoken when he wanted to be and enjoyed taking part in local politics but where his wife was concerned he usually gave in to her plans if only for the sake of peace.

All the members of the Rodrigas family were looking forward to the carnival festivities. Miguel, a well-built, muscular young man of eighteen, was captain of the local football team and there was to be a football tournament between visiting teams. He had always enjoyed participating in sporting activities and was popular among his cronies who respected his confidence and quick sense of humour. His smile came readily to his face, showing the gap in his front teeth, not quite as obvious as it used to be, now that he was attempting to grow a large moustache like his father's.

Sixteen-year-old Pedro was also stockily built with a thatch of hair that was jet black and eyes of the same colour. He had offered to supervise the fireworks on the morning of the feast of St Joseph the Worker and was also driving one of the floats.

Jose on the other hand had a different reason for looking forward to the festival; he would be able to spend some more of his time with Velana. She was in his thoughts constantly. He was deeply in love with her and could hardly concentrate on anything else but his darling Velana.

The church hall began to fill up. Mamma Maria was in her element as she got everyone organised and into their places for choir practice.

Father Silvas walked through the archway of the walled garden and looked up at the night sky. The moon was full, millions of stars flickered like tiny candles in the great dome of the heavens, otherwise all was still, the sound of organ music drifting from the hall only adding to the sense of serenity that was everywhere.

This was a favourite time of day for Father Silvas, he loved to stroll through the garden in the evening and to be with himself and his own thoughts.

The garden was his pride and joy. In his spare time he enjoyed working in it and could sometimes be seen, perched at the top of a ladder, half-hidden among the branches of the apple trees, pruning and snipping. It was he who put out the border plants, blending colour into harmonious arrangements, one into the other, purple lupins and blue iris, cloudy white spiraea, scarlet poppies, pink rose-scented peonies.

All this was achieved despite being bent double

sometimes with rheumatism, his body twisted and gnarled into something resembling the shape of his own apple trees. But he was tough of mind and spirit with a face full of character, and steel grey eyes that were shining now as he listened to the choir. They were all in good voice tonight he thought, especially the sopranos, whose bell-like voices rang out into the night air, but there was one voice in particular that stood out above the rest, powerful and sweet, singing in harmony – Velana's lilting voice, one that touched the emotions of everyone who heard it.

Father Silvas was no exception. He smiled as he listened; closing his eyes he kept time to the music by tapping his fingers on top of the wrought-iron gate.

He pictured Maria Rodrigas keeping a strict eye on everyone, making sure that everything was going smoothly. He was in control of what went on in and around the church but he believed in designating a share of the workload among his parishioners, especially people like Maria, God bless her. She had always found great joy in working for the church and furthering its function in the community.

Father Silvas took a deep breath, inhaling the fragrance of the garden as he ambled along the path towards the church hall, his dark clothing in contrast to his snow white hair shining in the moonlight.

Under the watchful eye of his mother Jose had tried to make himself look busy, lifting and arranging seats, helping with the tables, but all the time his only thought was to be near Velana and he made sure he was standing next to her during choir practice.

He had a good tenor voice and as they sang together, their voices blending in harmony, he took her hand to squeeze it gently. Velana felt a fiery tingling surging deep inside at his touch and the pink colour rose into her cheeks. She looked radiant and felt wonderful and wanted to tell the world about her love for Jose Rodrigas but they both knew they would have to try and keep their passionate feelings for each other a secret . . .

But the expression in their eyes when they looked at one another, the entwining of their hands, didn't go unnoticed.

Father Silvas, coming in from the garden to quietly slip into a corner and listen to the singing, saw the gesture of affection between the two young people. It was no surprise to him, however. He had already observed the look on Velana's face whenever Jose was near. She bloomed and glowed like a star in the night and everything about her seemed to radiate light.

Father Silvas had witnessed the look many times throughout his long years and knew it was the look of a woman in love.

But there was a troubled sadness in the old priest's eyes as he sat there in the shadows of the hall. Jose had served mass with him for many years as an altar boy; there was a goodness in him, he possessed special qualities, and Father Silvas had always encouraged him to follow the church and indeed had groomed him for the priesthood for he knew in his heart that the boy had a calling for the clergy.

He had often talked it over with Jose's parents, Miguel Rodrigas senior and Maria, and they had all thought the same, that someday he would join the Holy Order and train to be a priest.

At this moment in time, however, Father Silvas had other things to think about. The committee ladies had a lot of little problems to sort out and wanted his advice on matters pertaining to the coming festival – things like the arranging of flowers; the number of floats that would be required; the cooking of the meals for visiting clergy; the dressmaking and sewing of costumes, et cetera. The list was endless, Father Silvas listened patiently as the women talked. He knew everything would fall into place on the day; he had great faith in the committee and knew he could rely on each and every one of them to do their very best to make it a gala occasion.

Maria had been unusually silent for the past few minutes. It was obvious that she had something on her mind and when the others stopped talking she cleared her throat and said, "Father, we know that you have always led the procession in the past by walking up the valley, through the town and back to the church, quite a long way to go, especially the steep hill up to the town, so this year we would all like you to ride on this special buggy that Pedro has designed and built for you. It's powered by batteries and runs very silently so it won't disturb you when you're thinking."

At that moment Pedro came through the kitchen door, sitting on a little four-wheeled car which he drove round the hall in a full circle, manoeuvring it between people and chairs. "Come on and sit on it, Father, and try it out," cried Pedro, his dark eyes flashing with excitement. "You'll find it easy to drive. I put it together with parts of two old scooters and bits of old washing machines. It even has a light at the front and a musical horn so people will know when you are coming to visit."

"You're a genius Pedro, it certainly looks a fine machine," said Father Silvas, his face sparkling as he climbed aboard and sat on the comfortable seat that had been salvaged from an old bus.

"Well, Father," said Pedro, "I thought to myself if the Pope can have a Pope-mobile surely you can have a priest-mobile to get you around the garden and wherever you want to travel."

Father Silvas pressed the musical horn and the 'Bells of St Mary's' rang out; he pushed the gear stick forward and the little car moved off around the hall, Pedro walking beside him to show him what the switches and levers were for. The old priest, happy at last at being mobile, was smiling with delight as he moved through his flock, some of whom had tears in their eyes at the sight of him and how comfortable he looked sitting in his little car.

"God bless you all," he cried as he drove around the hall and out through the front door, slowly getting used to the controls, Pedro alongside, explaining how the batteries could be charged up each night from the mains and that it would run for approximitely twenty kilometres on one charge.

"How clever and compassionate you are, Pedro," said Father Silvas. "There will be a special place in heaven for you someday. God bless you, my son," he added as he moved off through the archway and along the path of his beloved garden sighing with contentment as he stopped every now and then to sniff in the luscious fragrance of the flowering rose-beds, their varying hues of pink, yellow, and white showing bright in the moonlight.

Chapter Three

On special feast days the church drew a stream of life from the farms and villages surrounding the little town of Olhão. For some it was a spiritual calling, for others it was the feeling of being needed and wanted within the church, which had always been a gathering place for social events in Portugal.

It had been three weeks since the committee meeting, when a number of decisions had been made for the festival. Now the big day was here, the day of the feast of St Joseph the Worker, and the usually quiet streets of Olhão were alive with bustle and colour.

The crowds had waited impatiently for the floats to start moving and now they were coming along. Velana was on one of them, standing beside the other members of the choir, surrounded by garlands of flowers. She could see Jose leading the way, walking beside Father Silvas who was sitting on top of his little car dressed in his robes.

Pedro had already set off the rockets high above the town, the loud thunderous bangs adding to the excitement everywhere. The procession moved forward, the choir started to sing, the sound of their voices soaring out joyfully.

"Ave, Ave Maria." Father Silvas chanted the blessing as he passed.

All along the way, doors and shutters were opening,

people coming out to bless themselves before joining the human crocodile that had tagged on behind the floats. It was a moving and happy occasion and a way of life for the country folk who had put their trust in God.

Theresa and Mario Domingo walked along together holding hands. Mario hadn't been very well lately; the local doctor, Valdez, had examined him and had thought it might just be overwork but had told him that he wanted a specialist to look at him just to be on the safe side. Meanwhile, the doctor had recommended rest for Mario, and Theresa had tried her best to make him take things more slowly, not an easy matter as he had always thrived on work and found it difficult to sit still for any length of time.

Maria held on tightly to her husband's hand as they strolled up the dusty road, following the parade, honouring St Joseph the Worker who centuries before had come to this valley to spread the word of God among the people and to teach them about the fruit-growing potential of the land.

The knowledge had been handed down through generations of country folk who had worked and cultivated the land to bring it to its present-day abundant growth: golden sweet-smelling oranges; almonds ripening in the sun; big yellow lemons clustering together so thickly it was difficult to see the dark green foliage.

The countryside in early summer was made up of light and dark with the sun casting soft shadows on the red earth and the gold-tinted leaves swaying against the deep blue of the Portuguese sky, the trees running up the valley in patterns of brightness and shade interspersed by white houses and farms that were dazzling in the sun's spilling rays.

* * *

The parade had ended at the church square in the town and some of the men began to drift off to watch the football match. Miguel junior was playing centre foward and Farmer Rodrigas and Pedro were eager to get to the pitch for kick-off time.

"Don't you be drinking too much," Maria warned her husband. "You know what it does to you, it makes you sleepy and tired and you've got to watch your blood pressure."

"Don't worry, Maria, I won't drink at all," he answered glibly, running his fingers through his luxuriant moustache, "I just want to see the game. The two teams are finalists so it should be an exciting match and if Miguel's lot win they will be through to the regional finals."

"We'll see you later, Mamma," said Pedro. "And don't worry," he added with a mischievous grin, "I'll make sure Papa behaves himself."

They each gave Maria a quick peck on both her cheeks and moved off into the busy throng.

The choir had finished singing and Velana was about to climb down from the flower-bedecked float when she felt strong arms around her, lifting her down to the ground.

It was Jose, his dark eyes flashing a loving smile as he kissed her lightly on the cheek. He had just come out of the church vestry where he had changed into an open-necked white shirt and blue shorts. He looked casual and handsome and Velana's heart missed a beat when he whispered, "Let's go down by the river, I want to be alone with you for a while."

He held her hand tightly as they made their way over the rough cobbles of the town square and down towards the old stone bridge whose four broad arches spanned the River Ola. It was a secluded place, popular with young lovers who wanted to be by themselves for a while. Great banks of rock made good seating and eating places, making it an ideal spot for picnickers.

It was cool and shady, the clear water of the river lapped against the bank, producing a comforting gurgling sound. Jose took Velana's hand and placed a soft teasing kiss on her fingers in a gesture of intimate relaxation.

"I can't forget that night in the poppy field," he told her softly. "I keep thinking of you, how lovely you are, how good it was with us." He kissed her hungrily and with a little moan she melted against his warm body, her breath coming in short gasps as he pushed up her blouse and ran his hands over her breasts, feathering her nipples with his fingertips.

"Oh Jose, I remember that night, too," she murmured hoarsely against his mouth. "I haven't been able to settle since, I want you always to make love to me."

He saw the desire in her eyes and gently he unbuttoned her dress and let it drop to the ground. He kissed her again, over and over, whispering tender endearments in her ear, burying his face into her flowing blonde hair, his hands moving over her body, making her shiver with delight.

"Velana, my own sweet darling," he breathed huskily, lowering his dark head to kiss the young slopes of her breasts, his mouth moving downward to nuzzle the soft mound of her belly, making her sigh and whimper with pleasure. She could feel him struggling out of his shorts, shaking off his shirt and she opened her eyes to see him standing naked in front of her.

"Jose," she whispered, running her hands over his bronzed skin. "I love you."

"I love you too, Velana," he answered quietly and a

soft wild cry came from her lips as he smothered her with kisses and buried his face in her breasts, pushing her gently to the soft, grassy earth.

After that it was just the two of them, locked in their own world of ecstasy and when it was over they lay back, holding one another, not moving or speaking, content for a while to be still and quiet and peaceful.

Slowly the sounds of the outer world came back to them: the river lapping against the bank, a small bird chirping and calling for its mate.

Velana stirred and ran her fingertips over Jose's face, making little circles at his temples, running them through his thick dark hair. "You are my love," she whispered softly, "my one and only love forever."

They held each other for a long time, in a gentle lovers' embrace, both of them lost in the wonder of their feelings for one another, surrounded by an aura that made everything around them seem lighter and brighter and somehow utterly magical.

Chapter Four

It was two minutes to go to full time and the teams had drawn one goal each after a hard-fought match. Miguel came running down the wing. He was about forty yards out after dribbling round and beating off a defender. He had noticed that the goalie was a bit off his line and he unleashed a left foot shot that came in like a thunderbolt, giving the rest of the defenders and the goalie no chance as the ball almost burst the net. The crowd responded in rapturous applause and uproar.

"Goal! Goal! Goal!" The cry echoed round the field; Miguel senior and Pedro were jumping up and down with excitement and joined the surge forward onto the park as the referee blew the whistle for full time.

Miguel junior was the hero of the day and was hoisted onto the shoulders of his team mates and carried round the field in a lap of honour, all of them singing a triumphal song at the top of their voices.

The crowd joined in the singing, someone spotted Miguel's father and brother and they too were hoisted up to join in the parade and all of them went marching up the dusty road towards the town where the celebrations were still in full swing with people dancing and singing and generally having a good time.

Caught up in the excitement, some members of the winning team decided to go for a swim in the local fountain that stood in the middle of the square and soon they were standing on top of the bronze statues of mermaids that circled the well, splashing each other merrily and shouting for Miguel who was still being carried around the square.

As he came past the fountain he balanced himself on top of his team mates' shoulders and with a cry of bravado he performed a neat somersault into the water to the delight of the onlookers who grinned at the sight of him splashing and floundering about.

Seeing his chance, Pedro slipped away. It would be dark soon and he wanted to get things ready for the evening fireworks display.

Maria and Theresa had been busy helping out at one of the stalls, serving cool drinks and coffee to the tourists and visitors. "Let's sit down and have a moment to ourselves," Theresa suggested during a quiet spell.

"Good idea," Maria agreed, "take the weight off our feet – my bunion is killing me," she added as she sat down to take off her shoes and rub her swollen ankles.

Theresa poured two coffees and they leant back and relaxed, but weren't left alone for long. Everyone was gathering to watch the fireworks display and Farmer Rodrigas, Jose and Velana, Mario and Father Silvas, came out of the crowd to sit down beside the two womenfolk.

It was night now, lights from street lamps and shop windows were spilling out, deep shadows lay across the cobbled square. Jose held Velana's hand underneath the table; his touch was warm and comforting and she responded by gently stroking his palm.

Father Silvas coughed; he didn't address anyone in particular when he said, "I've just received news from Paris in a letter from the Bishop who runs the training school for young priests. After careful consideration, and with the references I sent to him, Jose has been accepted to train for the priesthood and can leave for Paris almost immediately."

Maria's face lit up; she blessed herself and kissed the old priest's hand. "Oh thank you, Father," she said hoarsely, "God bless you." She looked at Jose with tears in her eyes. "My son, my dear, dear son," she cried, "I'm so proud of you." Then turning to her husband she added, "Did you hear that, Papa? Our son is going to be a priest."

Her husband stroked his large moustache and smiled a beaming smile. "I heard, Mamma, every word that Father Silvas said. It's wonderful news and is just what we have always wanted for Jose."

Velana was speechless, her body went rigid, her head started to swim. She held on to Jose's hand under the table, clutching it till her knuckles turned white, then, as the full import of the old priest's words really hit her, she felt her whole being go weak and limp.

She couldn't look at Jose, her eyes filled up with tears. At that very moment the first rockets exploded in the night sky in brilliant sunbursts that formed spectacular patterns and colours before cascading down to earth in breathtaking arches of light. After that they came one upon the other in blinding flashes, illuminating the sky, shining on the upturned faces of the spectators – reflecting the tears on Velana's cheeks . . .

She could stand it no longer. Struggling to her feet, stifling the sobs racking her body, she ran into the crowd and soon became lost from sight.

"Velana!" Jose jumped up and made to go after her but Maria caught hold of his arm. "No, son," she advised quietly, "let her be alone for a while. She'll need time to come to terms with the news she has just heard."

"But I must see her, Mamma!" he burst out in an agony of feeling. "I can't leave her like this!" Breaking away from his mother's grasp he plunged into the crowd to go after Velana.

Mario nudged Theresa and whispered, "I think we'd better make our way home. Velana is very upset, we must be with our little girl."

Theresa smiled sadly and nodded. She remembered the night her daughter had come home late after seeing Jose. She had been glowing, she'd had that look about her of a young woman who had discovered love for the first time and ever since then there had been a sparkle in her eyes at the very mention of Jose's name.

Theresa turned to Maria. The two women looked at one another for a long time before putting their arms round each other in a comforting embrace. "Our young people are growing up and making their place in the world," Theresa said softly. "Life can be wonderful, it can also be very cruel. In the end it will all be for the best but that doesn't stop the suffering in between."

Maria nodded. "Life is for living and our children have to learn to take the rough with the smooth. You and I have always been friends and always will be, whatever happens. My son and your daughter have grown up with one another; theirs was a special friendship from the start, now it has grown into something a little bit more. But Jose has a calling, you understand that, Theresa, it was meant for him, just as something else is meant for Velana, something that will be right for her also."

"I understand," answered Theresa calmly, though her heart was aching for the hurt she knew her daughter must be feeling at that moment.

Two terrific explosions, the roar of the crowd, signalled the end of the fireworks display; there was silence for a little while, then the sound of guitar music went echoing through the square, filling the air with rhythm and song.

Velana was already home in the farmhouse by the time Theresa and Mario arrived. She had got a lift on one of the haycarts returning up the valley and didn't know that Jose had gone after her when she had left everyone so hurriedly.

She was sobbing ceaselessly, lying on top of her bed, devastated by the turn of events that night.

Mario took three cups out of the kitchen cupboard and laying them on the table he busied himself preparing coffee. Theresa went into Velana's little bedroom. It was dark except for the beam of light coming from the kitchen doorway. Theresa sat down beside Velana and stroked her long, flowing, blonde hair.

"Oh, Mamma, what am I to do? I love him so!" Velana cried as she buried her head in her mother's bosom.

Theresa held her daughter in her arms and whispered, "There are many kinds of love, my dear, dear child. The love of father and mother, brothers and sisters, husbands and wives – the love of the church. Some of us are gifted and chosen to serve God in this world. Caring and sharing God's compassion and love with all others. It takes a very special person who can light up a room the way Jose does when he enters, with an aura and warm glow coming from him. Father Silvas recognised that special quality and gift and knew in his heart that Jose was truly a chosen one for the priesthood. That is why he must leave soon for France to start his training – and why you have to be strong and let go of him with your blessing."

Velana stopped sobbing, and turning, she looked up into her mother's eyes and whispered, "It's very hard to see it that way just now. Give me a little time and

I might be able to understand it better, Mamma. Right now it hurts so deeply!" Crossing her hands over her chest she sighed a deep sigh, the tears streaming down her face.

"There, there, sweetheart, I think I know something of what you are feeling," Theresa said soothingly. "Let the tears flow, but try and think of your inner strength, you are a very unique person also and you too have magical qualities. I am your mother, remember, I know what you are made of. You're my special girl and nothing can keep you down for very long . . ."

They were both startled by a crashing sound coming from the kitchen. Jumping up they ran through the narrow doorway to see Mario lying sprawled on the kitchen floor, surrounded by broken cups and dishes. He had fallen backwards; a little pool of blood was forming where he had struck his head on the floor.

"What's happened . . . Papa?" cried Theresa. "Oh, dear God! What have you done? Kneeling down beside him she turned him on his side and tried to revive him but it was no use; he remained unconscious. "Quick Velana," she threw over her shoulder, "run and phone for Valdez! I think it's serious."

Velana slipped her feet into her sandals and raced like the wind, away from the house and down the dusty moonlit road to the phone box at the crossroads.

Left alone, Theresa loosened her husband's tie and belt and held him in her arms. "Oh, please, Mario, don't let it be like this!" she cried out in anquish, "don't leave me."

Mario's eyes flickered for a moment and then his body went into spasms, his arms and legs jerking and shuddering for what seemed an eternity before he stiffened and lay still, the life ebbing from his wracked body.

"The doctor's on his way, Mamma!" Velana uttered breathlessly as soon as she was back inside.

"Velana, my sweetheart, it's too late for the doctor, we'll have to send for Father Silvas, your father is gone." Theresa was sobbing as she held her husband in her arms, rocking him to and fro, to and fro.

Velana was stunned into silence, she couldn't believe her father was dead, it had all happened so quickly. Her head was in a turmoil. How could he leave them like this? So suddenly? One moment he was making coffee, the next he was lying dead on the floor. The tears were welling up inside her but she choked them back. She had to be strong for her mother's sake. She blessed herself and once more ran out through the door and down the dusty road to the call box, only this time it was to phone for the priest.

Chapter Five

The news spread through the valley like wildfire. Mario Domingo had passed away. No one could believe it. The folk in the town and surrounding villages stood at their doors and talked about it in hushed voices. They had known him all their lives. He was part of the scene, part of a pattern that was familiar and dear to them.

The Rodrigas family were shocked when they heard the sad tidings and were filled with concern for Theresa and Velana. The practical side of Maria's nature was quick to surface. No good moping around, help would be needed in the Domingo household and soon she, her husband, and her three sons were making their way up the valley to pay their respects and help in any way they could.

It was mid-morning as they entered the little farmhouse. Everything was shining and clean – spic-and-span – and nothing looked amiss except for the black clothes that Theresa and Velana were wearing and the dark shawls covering their heads.

As they all embraced one another Jose gazed at Velana's pale face framed in the black shawl. She looked more beautiful than he had ever seen her and taking her hand he held it for a long moment as he kissed her gently on the cheek. He looked into her eyes and she held his gaze; something deep and new and wonderful passed between them, a bond of lasting and loving friendship, something that they knew would remain with them to the end of their lives.

Velana sensed a deep, warm, comforting aura coming from Jose, a glow that somehow lightened her heavy heart. He was so different from anyone else she knew, he would always stand out in a crowd, so tall and proud was he, so much an individual in every way. She had always felt strong whenever she was near him and some of his strength reached out to her now, making her want to share with him the things that were dearest to her heart, even those that were laden with sadness.

Taking his arm she whispered, "Come and see Papa", and led him into the next room.

A high bed with brass ends stood in the middle of the room and in it lay Mario, dressed in his Sunday best suit, his hair and beard neatly combed, his hands folded peacefully across the bible on his chest.

Jose blessed himself and leaned over the bed to kiss him on the forehead. His skin was cold as marble. "Your papa's asleep now, Velana," Jose whispered softly. "He has gone to the Eternal Light and now he's at peace."

Velana nodded; she knelt in front of the bed and all the loving thoughts she had about her father came rushing back to her, together with memories of herself as a little girl when her papa was never far from her side, teaching her and guiding her in the ways of the world.

He had been such a knowledgeable man and had shared with her some of the many secrets that only he knew, all about plant life and fruit growing, fermentation and distillation. She had helped him strip the raw ingredients into the large pots to allow them to slowly ferment, and afterwards they had ladled the liquid into the stills with the log fires burning underneath to keep it at the right temperature.

He would say to her, "Keep the cooler filled up with

water, Velana, while the liquid condenses and drips out from the end of the worm." And he would nudge the log fire with his boot and the extra heat would make the raw spirit flow gently and clearly into the wooden casks for storage.

Afterwards she had loved sticking the labels onto the barrels, now filled with different kinds of spirits and essential oils for medicinal purposes, and, using her best writing, she would enter all the details into the ledger for the records.

When they made lavender oil they didn't have to go through the process of fermentation but simply put the freshly-cut stalks and flowers straight into the stills. When the oil began to flow the beautiful fragrance of lavender hung in the air like nectar and wafted all around in the soft evening breezes blowing up the valley.

When the day's work was done her father would sit in the porch, painting and carving his little icons while she sang to him, mostly songs of country and village life though she had a natural talent to sing any type of song. She only had to hear a melody once or twice and she could hum and sing it note perfect and her papa would say, "Velana you have a perfect ear for music, it is a gift from God and you must never neglect to use it."

Throughout her young years he had encouraged her in every way he knew how and had bought her first guitar for her when she was only seven. It wasn't long before she could play the chords to almost any tune. His favourite was 'Plaisir d'Amour', the song of love, and when she had finished playing he would say, "Everyone in the world should be loving and kind to each other."

Velana remembered how he used to take Mamma's hand and hold it firmly to his chest and how he had looked at her – the devotion and love shining out of his eyes – then he would place his latest carving in front of her for her approval and she would gaze at it with pride and say, "You're the kindest, most loving man in the whole wide world, and everyone in the valley respects you."

And now he was lying here, in this bed, unmoving and cold, all the warmth, all the life, departed from him.

Velana's throat tightened, her eyes brimmed with the tears of her sorrow. How could she bear it? How could she live without her papa at her side? Never to know again his selfless love, his pride and joy in all her small achievements . . .

"Velana, come away now." Jose placed his hand under her elbow and helped her to her feet. They could hear unfamiliar voices in the next room and strange bumping sounds, as if the furniture was being moved around, and then suddenly two men appeared – the undertaker and his assistant – carrying the empty pine coffin through the doorway and into the bedroom of Mario Domingo.

Chapter Six

The little butterfly fluttering and hovering outside the shuttered window caught Theresa's eye as it danced in the air with gossamer wings, delicately casting its tiny shadow through the slats in the shutter.

It had been two days since Mario had died and this was the morning of the funeral. The farmhouse was filled with family relatives, townspeople and neighbours from around the countryside. Some of them had been here all through the night, praying silently in a candle-lit vigil, the only form of lighting to be allowed when there was a death in a house in southern Portugal.

Complete silence had been observed until it had become almost unbearable but now Father Silvas was standing at the head of the coffin saying the rosary, the mourners answering him fervently, "Holy Mary, Mother of God, pray for us sinners, now and at the hour of our death. Amen."

Theresa and Velana were kneeling at the foot of the coffin, leading the answering prayers. Velana stood up and Theresa thought how tall and fair she looked beside her dark-skinned relatives who were quite small in stature, like most of the local country folk.

She's like a pearl among olives, thought Theresa, her heart filling with pride for the daughter who had brought her such joy and support since the day she was born. Velana had always coped well with the hard work of the farm and very seldom complained, even when she was tired and disipirited which wasn't very often as she had great stamina and resilience of spirit.

Father Silvas gave the signal and the men carried the coffin out into the sunlight and placed it in the waiting carriage which was bedecked with flowers. It moved off, pulled by two mules, followed by the entourage of mourners escorting Mario on his last journey to the little churchyard overlooking the small town.

It was a double blow for Velana, the passing of her father, and Jose leaving for France that very evening. Her mind felt numb and cold but she knew for her mother's sake she had to be strong. Jose came to say goodbye to her later that day. A few of the relatives were still there, sitting round the table, talking and drinking little glasses of the local spirit medronho. Although they were well-meaning they were becoming a bit loud. Velana's head was buzzing with the babble of noise they were making and she was glad to take Jose out into the garden where it was peaceful and quiet.

Now that the moment of parting had come she wanted it to be all over quickly. Very soon Jose was going out of her life and the thought of that was almost too hard to bear. She was afraid that she would break down in front of him, beg him to stay, tell him that if he loved her as much as she did him he couldn't possibly leave her like this, especially after the death of her father, a time when it seemed to her as if her whole world had shattered around her.

But she didn't do or say any of these things; instead she took a deep breath and taking his hand she placed a little silver cross in his palm and whispered, "I want you to keep this forever; it will protect you, and . . . I hope it will remind you of me whenever you look at it."

His dark eyes burned into hers. "I don't need anything to remind me of you, my one and only Velana. I'll treasure the memory of each moment we had together, now and for all time." Handing her a small box he went on huskily, "Open this after I've gone."

She laid her hand on his arm; he kissed her on the forehead and they clung to each other for a brief moment. Her heart felt as if it was breaking in two. She closed her eyes, and their love and everything that they had been to each other, flashed before her.

And then she sensed that he had moved away from her. When she opened her eyes he was gone. She was standing alone in the garden. It was as if it had all been a dream and she stood quite still and quiet for a long time before she remembered the little box he had given her.

Inside was a little prayer book and she stared and stared at it, her breath held tight and deep in her throat. "Jose." She whispered his name, the tears trembling on her lashes. She brushed her fingers through the pages and there, pressed into the middle of the book, were two bright red poppies, still with the fragrance of the summer fields lingering on their petals.

What seemed like raindrops fell onto the flowers, but it wasn't raindrops falling, it was the tears of Velana Domingo who had lost her childhood sweetheart.

Chapter Seven

The sound of a car engine coming up the road awoke Theresa with a start. She wondered who it could be. It was only seven-thirty in the morning, a time when most people were just getting up or concerning themselves with the affairs of the household.

Getting out of bed she pulled on her dressing-gown and opened the front door. Dr Valdez was standing in the porch, the same solemn expression on his face as on the night Mario had died, almost a week ago.

"I'm very sorry to get you up at this hour, Theresa," he said apologetically, "but I'm making my way to the next village and I had to see you on a matter most urgent."

"Come in, Doctor, and sit yourself down," urged Theresa. "Would you like a coffee?"

"No, thank you," said the doctor, taking the offered chair and sitting down on it rather heavily. "I'm really in quite a hurry so if you don't mind I'll come to the point right away. Firstly, I've seen the results of Mario's post-mortem and they don't look too good, I'm afraid. He died from a hereditary disease, one which is passed down through the family line . . ."

Theresa gasped. Collapsing into a chair she blessed herself and whispered, "Oh, no, my poor Mario, perhaps if he'd had treatment . . ." Her voice trailed away.

The doctor coughed and looked uncomfortable.

"Theresa, please prepare yourself for what I have to tell you next. It concerns your daughter and it's no use me trying to hide anything from you. There is every reason to suppose that your daughter has been affected by this illness; it is particularly dangerous to the females in the family and I'm here to suggest that Velana must undergo some tests so that treatment can be started at once.

"We have to try to ward off the disease with a new type of medication that the researchers in Lisbon have been working on. I urge you, Theresa, to pursue this matter with the utmost possible haste. Your daughter must be told immediately. She'll have to go into hospital, maybe for quite some time, even then there is no guarantee of a complete cure." He stared down at his hands and shook his head. "There must have been a history of the illness in the family, it's a wonder that no one has recognised it sooner."

Theresa stared at him and whispered hoarsely, "Mario's mother and grandmother and all his aunts and sisters died very young but no one knew it was a hereditary disease. They passed away in different circumstances at different times, all premature deaths which the family accepted as God's will."

Dr Valdez leaned over and took her hand in a firm grip. "Well, it's out in the open now, Theresa, and if anything can be done to save Velana then we must do everything in our power to see that it happens."

Velana was in the next room. She had been bathing herself and washing her hair when Dr Valdez's car had come bumping up the road. Drying herself she wrapped her hair in a towel and after hastily pulling on her clothes she was about to go through to the living room when some of the doctor's conversation with her mother came filtering through to her.

At first she thought they must be talking about someone else, someone whose father had a family history of some sort of terrible illness. Then she heard her mother speaking her father's name, telling the doctor about a hereditary disease that had run in the Domingo line for generations . . .

A wave of nameless dread engulfed Velana. The colour drained from her face, her pulse began racing so fast she thought she was going to faint. "No, Papa," she whispered, "oh, please, no . . ."

She stood staring at the door knob, biting her lip, fighting back a wave of nausea that was rising within her, then with a shake of her head she forced herself to turn the knob and go through into the next room.

"Velana." Theresa half rose but her daughter motioned her to sit down again.

"I heard, Mamma." Despite her pounding heart, Velana's voice was quiet and controlled, "Everything the doctor said." Turning to him she went on, "I'm sorry, Doctor, this must be difficult for you, but I have to know when . . . what my chances are if I don't have treatment."

Dr Valdez returned her unwavering gaze. "Practically nil, I'm afraid; females with this illness don't live as long as the menfolk. Your father, God rest him, really had quite a long life, all things considered."

"When will I have to go into hospital?" Velana said in a strange, flat voice.

"As soon as I can arrange it. It's imperative that you start treatment as soon as possible."

"Will it be painful?" whispered Velana.

The doctor put his hand on her shoulder. "First things first, my dear child, better not to dwell on that side of it just now. In my opinion you've got enough to deal with for the moment. You've got spirit, Velana, I'm sure that alone will stand you in good stead for what lies ahead."

"But I feel so fit and healthy, doctor, I don't feel as if there is anything wrong with me." Velana's voice rose a little as blindly she sought the comfort of her mother's arms.

"Oh, dear God!" Theresa, who had been very silent for the last few minutes, released a sudden cry of anquish and hugging her daughter to her breast she said in a choked voice, "Oh my dear, dear, sweetheart, I never ever thought I would have to tell you this but your mamma has lived with a secret all the years of your life. Mario, your papa, God bless him, wasn't your real father. Your father was a Scottish seaman I met when I worked in the fish market in the port of Faro, before you were born – before I even met Mario."

Velana stared at her mother in utter astonishment, her eyes wide and blue in the pallor of her face. She could say nothing, it was too much; all of it was too much for her dazed mind to take in at the one time.

Dr Valdez, too, seemed momentarily lost for words, then he coughed and cleared his throat. "Well, this puts a different complexion on everything and I may say I'm delighted at the news. This is a very painful and revealing moment for you both and no doubt you will want to be alone to talk everything over. I have to be going now, anyway, but you know you can give me a call if you need me for anything." He looked at Theresa. "Your secret is safe with me. Now that it's out in the open it will be a burden off your mind. You and Mario – he must have been very devoted to you . . ."

Tears gleamed in Theresa's eyes. "Mario was a brave

and good man, Doctor, he was never anything else but loyal to me and he loved Velana as if she was his own child. He was a man who never flinched from anything he tackled and I am proud that he was my husband."

The doctor nodded. "Everyone in the valley admired Mario Domingo. He was a great example in the community and renowned for his tact and diplomacy. You were always a close-knit family; now that he has gone there is no reason for that to change. The things you have just revealed have been a shock for Velana but when she has had time to assimilate it all then you and she must draw even closer together in order to remain as happy as Mario would have wished."

"Thank you for all your help, Doctor, and for being so understanding," said Theresa as she followed him to the door to see him out.

He smiled and nodded and patting her on the shoulder he murmured, "Good luck and God bless," before making his way down the path to his car.

The noise of his engine revving up broke the silence once more and Theresa stood at the door, watching till the car disappeared round a bend in the road, then she turned to go rather unwillingly back into the house to face her daughter's inevitable questions.

Chapter Eight

Velana listened to the sound of the doctor's car fading into the distance and she took a deep breath as her mother came back into the room to sit down quietly on a chair close to her, the expression on her face both apprehensive and anxious.

"This has been a very strange time for me, Mamma," Velana said at once, "with Papa dying, Jose going away to Paris . . . and now . . . this. I'm beginning to think the whole world has gone crazy and nothing is the same any more."

"I know, I know." Theresa put out a hand to stroke her daughter's hair. "But nothing stays the same, Velana; it can go on for years being the same and then – suddenly – the changes come, in your case one after the other, like a tide that can't be stemmed. I had to tell you about your real father. I was going to anyway when I thought you were grown up enough to be able to take it. I never dreamt it would be like this, when you've already been through so much, but circumstances made me speak much sooner than I'd intended . . ." Her voice broke, she bowed her head, and Velana saw the little white hairs gleaming at her temples.

"Oh, Mamma!" The cry was torn from Velana and putting her arms round her mother she held her close to her heart. "Please don't worry; you're the best mamma in the whole of the world and I know you would never deliberately do anything to hurt me. Just tell me, please, about – my real father. I want to know everything about him," she finished hesitantly.

Theresa gave a loud sniff. Taking her hanky from her apron pocket she blew her nose, straightened, and with a little shake of her head she said, "There, that's better, everyone should shed a few tears now and then, it does nothing but good."

She put her hanky back in her pocket and taking a shuddering breath she began to speak. "You want me to tell you about the man who was your real father, very well, I'll begin. His name was Ian McKinnon and he came from an island called Corrish on the west coast of Scotland. He was tall and fair with blue eyes like yours and so handsome I nearly die now just to remember him. I think I fell in love with him the moment I laid eyes on him, so strong, so full of life and laughter, so warm and loving."

Theresa, her eyes staring into space, was transported back in time as she went on. "His ship was in port for repairs and I met him when he came ashore. He used to bring fish for me to sell at my stall in the market and we'd go out on the town with the money we made. Oh, we had the most wonderful three weeks together. It was a whirlwind romance. We were so much in love it was as if we were the only two people in the world. He used to call me his 'little mermaid' and just swept me off my feet with all his compliments and talk. But it was over all too soon. His ship sailed away and I never heard from him or saw him again."

"Oh, Mamma! You must have been devastated!" The tears were spilling out of Velana's eyes. Her own heart was aching with emptiness for Jose and she knew only too well how her mother must have felt all those years ago.

"Yes, I was devastated, Velana, and when I found out I was pregnant I didn't know what to do or where to turn. I wanted to have the child of Ian McKinnon yet I was frightened of what people would say. It is easy in these parts to be branded a loose woman and I felt I couldn't speak to anyone about it. My parents were dead and it seemed I had nobody I could confide in.

"And then I met Mario, at a church social evening. He was so gentle and loving and caring. He knew I was going to have a baby but he still asked me to marry him. He loved me dearly and in time I fell in love with him too. You were born and our little family was complete."

Theresa paused for a moment, her eyes moist and sad. "The years passed, life for us all was good and sweet though of course we had our difficult times like everybody else. Mario was a wonderful husband and a devoted father. He was so proud of you, Velana, he accepted you as his own from the start. I never wanted anything to ruin our happiness and I put off telling you about Ian McKinnon. There didn't seem any point in raking up the past; now it has caught up with me and I'm afraid to look at you in case I see accusation and dislike in your eyes."

"Oh, Mamma!" cried Velana, her own eyes misty with emotion, "surely you know me better than that! You're my mother and I love you even more for the sadness and hurt you must have known when you were a young girl." Her eyes flashed suddenly. "But I tell you this, I will always think of Papa Mario as my father. Ian McKinnon is a stranger to me, one whom I will never meet, nor want to even if he is my flesh and blood."

Theresa stood up. "Fate is a very strange thing, Velana," she said softly. "Who knows what will happen in the future, we are all at the mercy of the twists and turns of life."

Velana said nothing. She had so much to think about. At the moment her mind could hardly make sense of the jumbled thoughts within it and with a sigh she rose to go and help her mother set the table for their belated breakfast.

The early morning sunlight was casting deep shadows across the distant hills; nearer to hand the dew was shining and glistening on the dark green ivy leaves surrounding the porch door where spiders had spun their silvery webs in every little nook and cranny.

Like the webs in our own lives, Velana thought, delicate yet strong, keeping us prisoners of our own circumstances just when we think everything is good and free and wonderful.

She looked across the shimmering valley where creamy grey stone walls edged the bright green fields. As the sun touched and awakened them, she could see the rich plain of many-coloured meadows stretching away to the distant hills and the blue mountains beyond.

It was good to sit here, doing nothing, a time of quiet withdrawal, a space of her own for just thinking and dreaming.

And then Maria appeared on the ridge of the dusty road, riding her ancient bicycle, a wide straw hat shading her from the bright morning sunlight, the casting shadows softening the light on her strong weather-beaten face, her plump figure held straight and erect as her feet went round and round in a rhythmic motion.

As she drew close to the Domingo farmhouse she looked up and waved to Velana sitting at the window. Maria knew that there was always an open door and friendliness awaiting her here. Like her own place it was a little isolated, surrounded as it was with fruit orchards and green fields, the windows like dark eyes looking out from the whitewashed walls under terracotta roof tiles that caught the radiance of the morning sunlight, everything reflecting the colour of the Portuguese sky, blue-shaded with hazy shadows under the trees.

"*Bonn dia*, Velana," Maria cried in greeting as she dismounted from her bicycle and pushed it up the path to the farmhouse porch. "That road seems to get steeper every time I come up here," she added, a little out of breath.

"*Bonn dia*, Maria, *como esta?* How are you?" Velana returned, smiling a little at the sight of Maria's hat sitting rather cock-eyed on one side of her head.

"I am as well as can be expected after that journey – and I only came because I have got something important to tell you. A film team has arrived in Olhão; they are doing a documentary film and the producer is looking for local singers to take part. The auditions start today and I took the liberty of putting your name down when I was in town yesterday. I couldn't get here any sooner and hope you'll be able to manage at such short notice."

"A film team!" Velana's eyes lit up at the news; turning to her mother she said excitedly, "Did you hear that, Mamma? Maria has put my name down for an audition!" Her hand flew to her mouth. "I'll never be ready in time. My best dress needs ironing and my guitar needs a first string! And how am I to get there on time? The donkey is out on loan, it's a long way to walk, I'll look terrible when I get there and I'll be so out of breath I won't be able to sing one note."

"Calm down, child," laughed Maria. "When you're ready you can borrow my bicycle. Your mother and me will sit and drink coffee and have a gossip till you get back."

After that Velana flew through the house like a tornado, doing her hair, pulling on her dress, fixing a string to her guitar, tuning it with hands that trembled slightly while Theresa and Maria stood by, handing her all the bits and pieces that she needed as she went along.

"That's me ready. How do I look?" she said at last as she finished brushing her hair.

"You look wonderful, a real little star," Theresa said proudly. "Take care going down the road – and God's blessings be with you, my dear, dear child."

"Off you go or you'll be late," Maria said impatiently. "Good luck – and remember to stay calm or you'll forget your words."

Both women watched as Velana mounted the ancient black bicycle and disappeared down the country road with her guitar strapped to her back.

Chapter Nine

"Velana Domingo." The name came clearly over the loudspeaker in the town square and there was a stir among the group of people waiting in the queue for their names to be called for the auditions that were taking place in the town hall.

One or two had already gone inside, now it was Velana's turn, and as she entered the hall and saw all the recording equipment set up, the butterflies in her stomach became so agitated she thought everyone must see how nervous she was.

Seated at a large table in front of the stage was one heavily-built, slightly balding, man, flanked by two young women who were busily taking notes and generally looking very efficient.

Velana went over and stood in front of the desk, not expecting to be noticed right away, she was pleasantly surprised therefore when the man looked up, smiled, and said, "Good morning. You're Velana Domingo, I believe. I'm Carlos Santos, the producer, and these are my assistants, Guida and Collette. Guida will accompany you on the piano to test your range and then you can sing anything you prefer."

Guida, well-dressed and sophisticated looking, led the way up the steps and onto the stage where she sat down at the piano. "Take your time, Velana," she said in a voice that was rich and warm. "Just try and sing these scales and I'll play for you."

Her fingers floated over the keys, blending major chords into minors, changing the keys from low to high octaves. Velana followed her every move, her resonant voice echoing all around the hall, as high and as clear as a bell.

Carlos Santos, who had been taking notes, stopped with his pen poised in mid-air to listen. "Ah, this is better," he whispered to Collette. "The best voice we've heard all morning. She's got perfect pitch and a wide range."

Guida was quick to notice the satisfied look on Carlos's face and she said briskly to Velana, "Right, what I want now is for you to sing one of your own songs. Anything you like."

Velana, feeling a bit calmer now, told the older girl that she would sing 'Plaisir d'Amour' in the key of G and strapping her guitar over her shoulder she started to sing the haunting melody. A hushed silence enveloped everyone in the hall. Workmen put their tools down and stood listening as the golden voice of Velana Domingo soared out, filling every corner with enchantment.

She finished the song to rapturous applause and shouts for more. Carlos got to his feet; he too was applauding, his face shining as he went marching up the stairs and onto the stage.

"Congratulations, my dear," he cried heartily, grinning from ear to ear. "You're the voice we've been looking for. It has taken a long time to find you, Velana Domingo, and I'm not going to let you slip through my fingers. I'd like to sign you up with a recording contract right away. I know this is all happening very fast but that's the way I operate if I see something I like. After we've finished filming here I'd like you to come to Lisbon with us. Guida and Collette will show you the ropes and fill in the details."

Velana pushed a strand of hair away from eyes that were round and big with excitement. She could hardly believe the evidence of her own ears. A recording contract! Just like that! She had always loved to sing and had hoped someday that she could perhaps make something of it. All through the years of her growing up, Papa Mario had told her that she had a voice that could take her places, but for it to happen like this, in the town hall in Olhão! It seemed too good to be true. Things like this didn't happen to a sixteen-year-old girl from a little farming community.

But it *was* happening. Carlos had just uttered the magical words; Collette and Guida were smiling at her as they waited for her to speak. A million questions rose to her lips but she was too stunned to utter a single one.

Guida saw her confusion and said quietly, "Would you like time to think about this, Velana? Perhaps sleep on it? It's a very big decision to make just at a moment's notice."

Velana hesitated. Guida was right. She couldn't just up and leave home at the snap of a finger; her mother needed her, there was always a lot of work to be done at the farm, especially now that Papa Mario was gone.

"I'll need to ask my mother," she said in a small voice. "My father died recently and all of this might be too much for her. If I went away she would be left on her own and – well – I'll have to see what she thinks before I can make up my mind."

"Would you like us to come home with you and explain it all to her?" Collette offered. "It would make sense for us to meet her anyway – just to let her see that you haven't been involving yourself in anything dangerous," she added with a laugh.

Velana nodded her agreement at the suggestion and after that she was left alone for a few minutes while the two women talked to Carlos, and then all three of them spoke to the remaining hopefuls waiting to be auditioned, telling them that they had found the singer they had been looking for and thanking them for sparing their time to be there that day.

There were a few groans and moans but one by one everyone began drifting away and Guida led Velana out into the town square where Collette was already sitting in the driver's seat of a sleek silver-coloured limousine.

"Your carriage awaits you, Velana," Guida said, smiling at the look of bemusement on the younger girl's face.

"But I can't go in this," Velana objected. "I rode here on Maria's bicycle and she'll be expecting me to come back with it."

"No problem, go and get the bike and we'll stick it into the boot of the car. It's big enough to take anything you like so take that worried look off your face and start enjoying all of this."

A few minutes later they were all settled in the car; Collette put it into gear and soon they were driving away from the town hall and the square, watched by the onlookers who nudged each other and nodded towards Velana sitting in the back of the opulent vehicle.

It was a vastly new and strange experience for Velana to be driven in such style through the familiar countryside. She was more used to donkey-drawn carts, bicycles, or just simply her own two feet, to get her around, and for the first few minutes of the journey she lapsed into silence, one in which she observed her new companions very carefully.

They were both impeccably dressed and well groomed. Guida, who was about twenty-five, was tall with jet black, short-cropped hair and a lovely open expression on her dark-eyed, creamy skinned face. The smart rust-coloured suit she was wearing, with matching shoes and handbag, was tailored to fit her elegant figure to perfection and she gave the impression that nothing could upset or ruffle her in any way.

Collette, who was smaller and plumper, was wearing a light blue suit with little white flashes at the collar and cuffs. She also had short dark hair but her large eyes were violet-blue, her skin golden brown, and though her personality was pleasant she seemed shyer and a bit more withdrawn than her colleague.

Velana, deciding it was time to ask some questions, spoke up suddenly. "Have you two worked together for very long?"

"We've both been with the same company for the past five years," Guida volunteered. "Mr Santos is a good boss. He's very fair and more or less leaves us to get on with our jobs and trusts us to see that things run as smoothly as possible. Collette is the business adviser and I'm the musical adviser, arranger, and talent spotter."

"You must have started early, to have a top job like that."

"I've been involved in music all my life, having begun training at the age of four. Both my father and mother were music teachers and it was always quite natural for me to be involved in what they were doing and to later recognise the gift in others. That is why, when I heard you singing this morning, I knew you had that special quality in your voice. I thought too, that when you sing, you seem to do it without your Portuguese accent and sound more like northern European."

Velana wasn't quite sure if that was bad or good and so she made no reply to the comment. Her voice couldn't possibly reveal the fact that she had family connections in Scotland. Family connections! It was the first time she had thought of it like that and she wondered if she ought to mention it. But no! It was too soon for any confidences like that. She had barely taken in the fact herself yet, let alone tell comparative strangers that her natural father lived in a remote island in Scotland and that he was as unaware of her existence as she had been of his until recently.

Scotland! That faraway land that she had only heard about in school and whose tiny place on the map seemed as distant to her as the moon in the heavens. What was it like, she wondered. Wet? Windy? Sunny? Warm? Or a combination of all the elements. Someone had once told her they had been there and it had rained all the time; they had also said it was beautiful, with mist shrouding the mountains and great white rivers foaming down through the valleys . . .

"Which way do we go now?" Collette's voice brought Velana out of her reverie.

"Turn left at the crossroads. Our farm is up there, at the top of the hill. In a minute you'll see the roof – and then we'll be home."

Chapter Ten

Theresa and Maria were sitting on the swing seat in the porch, drinking lemonade and fanning themselves with newspapers. Having talked themselves out, they were feeling drowsy and relaxed in the warmth of the afternoon sun. Through half-shut eyes they observed the lazy struttings and peckings of the chickens in the yard and watched the cloud shadows in the fields peacefully drifting along.

Theresa wondered how Velana was getting on and hoped she wouldn't leave it too late to start heading home on that old bike of Maria's with the steep hill to negotiate and the sun beating down on her back . . .

Of course, it all depended on how soon she was called in for her audition. These things took time, and though she didn't know very much about film people she had heard that they were strange creatures who shouted all the time and drank coffee by the gallon and maybe something stronger . . .

"There is a big silver car coming up the road and it is heading for your house."

Maria's startled voice jarred against Theresa's eardrums, lifting her out of a pleasant little afternoon siesta. "And the man in the moon might pay us a visit next week – if he has the time," Theresa returned, unable to keep a note of sarcasm out of her voice.

"No, really," persisted Maria. "Open your eyes and you will see for yourself."

"By the blessed saints!" Theresa could hardly believe it when she saw the limousine coming up the dusty road. "It must have lost the way, it can't be anything to do with us! But what if it is and here's me with my apron on!"

She began fumbling with her apron ties but it was too late, the car was drawing to a halt and people were piling out, and, amazingly, her own daughter was among them.

"Mamma!" Velana cried. "The audition was a success! I've brought Guida and Collette to meet you. We've got great news to tell you! I've been asked to sign a recording contract!"

Guida held out her hand; a very bemused Theresa took it rather tentatively. "I'm very pleased to meet you, Mrs Domingo," said Guida. "You've got a very talented daughter, her voice is perfect, just what we've been looking for, and yes, that's right, we would like her to sign up with us if that's OK with you."

Theresa was at a complete loss for words but Maria was perfectly capable of speaking for everyone. Taking a hand each of Velana and Theresa she clasped them to her bosom and said, "This is wonderful, wonderful news. I told you, Theresa, that something would happen for Velana that is right for her. I always knew that she would go places someday with that amazing voice of hers."

They did a little dance of celebration round the garden while Guida and Collette glanced round them appreciatively, struck by the tranquillity of the place, by the order of the endless rows of fruit trees running up the valley and the perfume of wild flowers drenching the air.

Theresa, recovered from the surprises of the last

few minutes, invited the visitors to stay for a meal which they willingly accepted, but first had to go down to the phone box at the crossroads to make a few business calls.

Velana and Maria busied themselves preparing the food but took a few minutes' break to have a glass of wine with everyone else. Theresa poured it into the crystal glasses that were only used for special occasions. Raising hers, she flicked her finger against the glass to make a chinking sound, the way Mario used to do, and then she looked at her daughter and said proudly, "To Velana, my wonderful daughter. May happiness and success follow you all the days of your life."

"To Velana!" The toast echoed round the room and she stood there, smiling round at everyone, her eyes big and blue in her flushed face, her blonde hair cascading down her back, not knowing what to say, her heart full to bursting in those emotion-fraught moments.

Then she burst out. "Oh, Mamma! How can I go away and leave you? Papa Mario is dead, you will be left on your own! I can't do this to you. I might be away for a long time."

"That's right," Collette nodded, turning to Theresa. "We want her to come to Lisbon with us. If everything goes well she'll be working there for some time and the farm seems quite a big place for you to manage on your own."

"That's no problem," Maria broke in eagerly, her round face pink with earnestness. "Miguel and Pedro are good boys, they'll help Theresa to look after things here and at harvest time the people from the local villages pull together and lend a hand where it's needed."

Guida smiled. "You seem to have a very good community spirit in these parts."

Maria nodded. "It all stems from the Church. We all

try to do God's work, and managing the land brings us close to him and to each other." As if to prove her point she blessed herself and went on, "How long are you going to be in our little town?"

"No more than a couple of days. We're doing some filming in the church and then we'll be off to Lisbon."

Velana, who had slipped away to see to the meal, came in at that moment, carrying a large casserole dish which she placed on the barrel-top table in the porch, beside plates of bread and cheese. The lid of the dish was removed, the steaming hot aroma of peaches poached in wine and honey wafted out.

"Mmm, it smells of nectar," Collette commented appreciatively and after that no one spoke very much as they were all too busy enjoying the simple but delicious meal out on the porch with the sounds of the countryside in their ears and the shadows growing longer in the valley.

Soon after they had eaten, the visitors took their leave, first removing Maria's bicycle from the car boot when she suddenly remembered it and enquired anxiously as to its whereabouts.

"We'll pick you up for rehearsals tomorrow," Collette said to Velana, "and we hope we'll see you all in church on our final day when we'll be filming the service. Thank you ever so much for the lovely meal. It was such a pleasure to meet and eat with you all and in such relaxed surroundings."

Guida echoed her sentiments and then they were off, driving down the dusty road, the shimmering heat of the day making the distant landscape look like a mirage.

"Well, I suppose I'd better be on my way, too," said Maria rather regretfully. "I'll have to get back to Miguel and the boys, they'll be wondering where I am and I've certainly got a lot to tell them. It's been a most unusual day altogether and I'm glad I was here to take part in it."

Theresa took hold of Maria and kissed her on both cheeks. "Thank you for all your help and company today."

"It's what friends are for," Maria returned cheerily. "Oh, don't forget to give Velana the letter that came while she was away."

Theresa gave an exlamation and withdrawing a letter from her apron pocket she handed it to her daughter.

The warm colour invaded Velana's cheeks. She had seen that writing before, in school, in all sorts of little jottings since.

"It's from Jose," Maria nodded. "There will be one for me too when I get home."

With that she hoisted herself onto her bicycle and went pedalling away at a leisurely pace, singing to herself, the words a bit distorted as she negotiated the lumps and bumps of the stony road.

Velana waited till she was in bed that night before opening her letter, her heart strange and sad within her as she read the words Jose had written.

'My Dear Velana,
    It seems such a long time since I said goodbye to you. How different life is here from the one I have known. The streets of Paris are full of bustle and noise and the valleys and farming communities of southern Portugal seem very far away.
    But if I shut my eyes I can see them vividly and I can picture you there among the fields and places of our childhood.
    I am happy here. Everyone is very kind and I

am kept busy with my studies and learning a little bit more every day about Christ's teachings.

This is my chosen path, Velana, and I am certain that you too will find the road that is right for you. I will never forget all that we meant to each other but know in my heart that we had to journey away from one another in order to find the spiritual strength to stand alone and separate as complete individuals. You will go forth and do great things, Velana Domingo, and I know I am going to hear about you and all that you have achieved.

May God bless you and hold you in His keeping.

Your loving friend. Jose Rodrigas.'

Velana lay on her back and held the letter to her breast. "Yes, Jose," she whispered into the darkness, "our journeys through life will take us away from one another, but you will always be with me, no matter where I go and what I do."

She fell asleep, still clutching Jose's letter, the tears drying on her pillow where they had fallen.

Chapter Eleven

Father Silvas wasn't too sure at first whether to let the film crew into the church. He was afraid they might do some damage with all the heavy equipment they carried around with them.

Carlos Santos told him they would pay for anything that might get broken though he gave every assurance that his crew were normally very careful about that sort of thing.

To further appease the old priest he even offered to do some repair work to the roof and bell tower, things that had needed doing for years; also to give a lick of paint to the interior of the building.

He was as good as his word. Father Silvas was really delighted when he saw the final results. The crew had worked around the clock to have everything ready on time and now the big day had arrived, the church was filled to capacity. Father Silvas had finished reading the gospel; he gave a slight nod of his head and the choir began to sing 'Ave Maria', accompanied by Guida playing the organ and conducting at the same time.

The wonderful sound was like a melodious wind blowing among woodland trees, it echoed through the church and touched the emotions of the congregation, leaving hardly a dry eye to be seen, as a starry-eyed Velana, standing alone in the aisle, sang the solo part, the camera team catching every moment on film.

Carlos Santos was delighted that all had gone so well. The crew had already filmed the surrounding countryside, interviewing local worthies and all sorts of other interesting people; the church service rounded everything off nicely and Carlos knew he had a winning documentary to sell to the TV companies.

As an added bonus he had found Velana; he knew she had that special quality that would make her a star, all it needed was for Guida and Collette to cultivate her finer points and the world would be her oyster. He could feel it in his bones and he was never far wrong where talent was concerned.

As mass finished, Father Silvas made his way through the sacristy and out into his beloved garden. He wanted to pick a bunch of his best roses and carefully he selected some of his most precious blooms and placed them in a yellow wicker basket lying in the back of his little priest-mobile. He then got into the driving seat and wended his way through the garden and round to the front of the church where the congregation had gathered outside and were congratulating Velana and the choir for the beautiful singing.

The old priest waited for a few moments before manoeuvring himself over to where Velana and her mother were standing.

"Velana, my dear," he said softly, taking both her hands in his. "I hear you are leaving us for pastures new. It will be a great experience for you and I wish you every success. God bless you, my dear child, I'll pray for you and hope you will always remember never to lose touch with your roots or your faith."

So saying, he handed her the basket of beautiful roses, on top of which lay a miniature missal prayer book with gold lettering.

"Oh, thank you, Father," Velana said, very touched

by the gesture. "What a wonderful thought, I'll cherish it always."

She opened it. On the first page he had written her name, followed by the words, '*Be good sweet maid and let who will be clever*, signed, Father Silvas.'

Velana looked up but he had already moved away, talking to the rest of his congregation as he guided his little car among them.

"I'm ready to go now, Mamma." Velana spoke with a little quiver in her voice as she experienced a feeling of apprehension now that the moment of departure had arrived. Guida and Collette were coming soon to pick her up and for her mother's sake she had tried to put a brave face on things. But as the seconds ticked away she was suddenly overwhelmed by the knowledge that for the first time in her life she was leaving home and all it meant to her.

Maria had promised that she would look in regularly to make sure that Theresa was managing and already she had work lined up for Miguel and Pedro that would ensure the smooth running of the Domingo farm.

Even so, Velana worried about her mother being alone, and she couldn't stop herself crying out, "Oh, Mamma, what am I to do? It's wrong of me to leave you like this! I'll miss you! I'll think about you all the time and wonder what you are doing."

Theresa had to smile a little at the look of tragedy on her daughter's face. "Hush, hush, Velana," she said soothingly, "everything's going to be fine. Of course I'll miss you too and all I ask is for you to look after yourself. Just remember how proud I am of you; this is your big chance so go out there and grab it with both hands."

She put her arms around her daughter and held

her for a long moment. There was silence between them and Velana was aware of her mother's heartbeat against hers, lulling her as it had done when she was just a child.

The spell of solace was broken by the sound of the limousine coming up the road and drawing up outside the farmhouse.

Between them, Guida and Collette helped Velana with her baggage and packed it all into the boot.

"I've made you each an apple and peach pie," Theresa said. "You can eat them on the journey if you feel a bit hungry."

"How kind and thoughtful you are," Guida said appreciatively. "And please don't worry about Velana. We'll look after her and won't let her out of our sight."

"We'll be with her night and day," affirmed Collette, taking Theresa's hand. "And I'll make sure she calls you regularly," she added as they began piling into the car.

"Bye, Mamma, take care." Velana hugged her mother briefly then she quickly turned away to hide her swimming eyes. She sat in the back seat, staring out of the rear window, waving to her mamma as they moved off down the road. The farmhouse got smaller and smaller as the wheels sped them away; her mother became just a dot in the distance, and finally disappeared from view.

Velana felt an emptiness in the pit of her stomach. She had done it, she had really left her mother and her home behind her for the first time in her life and she was unable to stop the tears from spilling over.

She thought of all the recent events in her life. The sad loss of Papa Mario; Jose leaving to go to France; the strange events leading up to the discovery that her natural father was a Scotsman living on a remote Hebridean island. Now she was on her way to Lisbon, or maybe even farther afield. Guida glanced at her sympathetically and squeezed her arm. "It will pass, Velana, for a while you'll feel a bit disorientated but you'll soon get the hang of things. I felt the same when I left home..." she grinned, "a million years ago now. I was miserable too – for maybe five minutes – but the adventure was bigger than anything else and now I only go home very occasionally as I'm too busy travelling the world with people like you."

"Me too," Collette added from the front. "We're big girls now, Guida and me, you're more of a baby but you'll soon catch up and just think, you're on your way Velana, the whole big crazy world is out there waiting for you and you're going to sock it to 'em with all you've got." She threw back her head and laughed, Guida did too, and Velana laughed louder than any of them in a burst of excitement that seemed to explode inside her like a fizzy bomb.

Collette was a good driver, unflappable, sure of every move she made, anticipating those of other drivers with instinctive ease. The car sped into the early morning traffic and up the motorway towards Lisbon.

When they had travelled a few miles, Velana fumbled in her pocket and taking out the little prayer book that Father Silvas had presented to her she placed it in a small box alongside the one Jose had given her before his departure for Paris. They both fitted snugly together. Somehow just looking at them made her feel better. She would keep them close to her always; she knew they would give her strength in the weeks and months and years to come.

Chapter Twelve

The taxi drove smoothly through the traffic along the Aveneda da Liberdade in the heart of Lisbon. A voice on the radio was singing, 'Que deus me Per-doe'. The taxi driver was whistling the tune and trying to keep time with the words of the song.

Velana sat in the back seat, listening and smiling, for the voice on the radio was hers. Three months had passed since she had left Olhão. It had been a hectic time for her, one that had passed in a whirlwind of engagements and recording sessions. She had been an overnight success, releasing one hit after another: 'Fa-Do Malhoa' 'Que deus me Per-doe' and 'Confesso' to name but a few.

She had topped the bill at the famous Tivoli Concert Hall the previous week and had brought the house down. Her name was on everyone's lips; it had all happened so quickly it felt like a dream.

Guida had been a wonderful help and influence on her, teaching her many things about dress and poise and how to handle herself in company, and stagecraft.

At heart she was still a country girl from a small farming community but now she was a star and belonged to the nation. That's what Collette had said to her after last week's show.

She felt as if she was floating in space and sometimes it seemed as if she had left the practical side of her nature back home, but through it all Guida and Collette were always there to give her advice and keep her on the right track.

At first they wouldn't let her out of their sight, but slowly, as her confidence grew, she started to make her own decisions about many things and the two older women began to relax a little and let her have more of her own way.

Today she had been shopping for some new clothes, one of the luxuries she was allowed to do on her own. She loved these shopping expeditions; it was so exciting being able to purchase anything she pleased without worrying about the price and it was so good to buy her mother a nice gift and have the store wrap it up and send it off.

On several occasions she had been recognised, someone only having to shout, "Velana! Velana Domingo!" for her to be surrounded and asked for her autograph, resulting in her having to eventually make her exit through a back door.

Now she was on her way to meet up with Guida and Collette at the home of Carlos Santos. The taxi turned into a quiet side street lined with trees. The houses were rather grand, elegantly painted and architecturally pleasing with archways leading into shadowed driveways. It was into one of these that the driver steered his vehicle, the tyres crunching on the gravel path as he drew to a halt outside a large three-storey villa.

The driver got out and opened the door for Velana, doffing his cap to her and executing a little bow as she emerged. She couldn't help smiling to herself at his formality but was careful to remember to give him a tip and to thank him when he saluted her before driving away.

A tall, thin woman in a severe grey and black dress

came down the front steps to extend her hand to Velana. "Good afternoon, Ma'am," she said in a plain but firm voice. "I'm the housekeeper. If you will come with me I'll escort you to your room."

Having relieved Velana of her boxes and shopping bags she led her up the steps and into the entrance hall, and from there they climbed up the graceful staircase leading to the second landing. The housekeeper opened a door at the end of the hall and ushered Velana into a charming bedroom at the back of the house.

The furnishings were of maplewood, the floors carpeted in pink and light blue, the windows curtained in pale pink silk. The bed quilt was of the same material, as were the lampshades and chair covers.

"What a beautiful room," Velana said a trifle nervously, the woman having reminded her of a fierce matron she had once encountered during a childhood sojourn into Faro.

"This is one of the special guest rooms, Ma'am," the woman said stiffly. "The other guests are downstairs with Mr Santos. If you would care to freshen up before joining them, the bathroom is through that door next to the window." At that juncture her face broke into a smile, transforming it completely. "If I may take the liberty, Ma'am, I have to tell you how much I enjoy your singing. It's a real pleasure to meet you and if there's anything you need just give me a ring on the intercom." With that she excused herself and left the room.

Delighted to be on her own for a time, Velana explored and inspected her surroundings. The bathroom was tastefully stocked with towels, shampoo, soap and bottles of bubble bath. Having satisfied her curiosity she looked at herself in the teardrop mirror on the wall and brushed out her long flowing blonde hair, wondering all the while who the other guests were and why they had all been invited to the home of Carlos Santos.

Everything was a bit of a mystery. Guida and Collette hadn't enlarged on the subject when she had asked them about it and, with the exception of the housekeeper, she hadn't seen anyone else since her arrival.

When she had freshened up, a mood of mischief seized her. Ever since leaving home she hadn't had much time for fun and games. It was all go from the moment she got up in the morning and from then on her day was mapped out for her.

It would make a change to break out occasionally and with a little intake of breath she decided that she would have a quick peep round the house before having to make an appearance downstairs.

Opening the door a crack she glanced out – and almost burst out laughing, for there waiting to escort her was the housekeeper, very upright and stiff, bristling a bit with her own importance.

Oh, well, it had been worth a try, Velana thought, as she followed the other woman down the staircase and through a maze of corridors, finally stopping at two large sliding doors which led into the main lounge.

With a controlled little flourish, the housekeeper slid the doors open and right away Velana was pounced on by Guida and Collette who were waiting to welcome her and introduce her to the other guests.

A slight hush had fallen as Velana entered the lounge and she felt her face growing warm as she wondered what was coming next. Mr Santos was standing at one of the windows, surrounded by some very distinguished-looking people.

"Ah, Velana," he called out as soon as he saw her, waving to make extra sure that she saw him. Making excuses to his guests he crossed the room and taking

Velana by the arm he led her to an elegantly-upholstered chair and told her to sit down.

"Rest and relax for a moment, young lady," he said with a nod. "How about a glass of sherry? There's nothing like it for calming the nerves and giving you a nice glow at the same time." Lifting a glass from a nearby table he handed it to her and stood over her, rocking gently on his heels and beaming at her in a fatherly fashion.

Velana didn't want to offend him. She had never liked sherry very much but to please him she took a sip and said, "Thank you, Mr Santos. This is a lovely house, you must enjoy coming home to it in the evenings after work."

"It's my pride and joy," he agreed. "After my dear wife, of course," he added, his eyelid coming down in a comical little wink.

Velana glanced round the room. It was large and comfortable, tastefully furnished with stylish plush chairs and sofas and some well-preserved nineteenth-century antiques. The curtains were of mulberry red brocade, indian rugs were scattered on the highly polished wood flooring, the walls were panelled and covered with impressionist paintings, and there was a beautiful barrel-fronted cabinet that stretched almost the length of one wall, filled with sparkling glass, fine china and silver. The top of it had been covered over with lace doyleys upon which trays of food had been laid out neatly for the buffet lunch.

"Ladies and gentlemen, can I have your attention, please?" Carlos Santos, having placed himself in a prominent position, held up his hand and spoke out loudly and clearly. One by one the voices died away and everyone stood around in groups to listen as he went on. "Most of you here are in the music and publishing business and have been invited to this special lunch to celebrate the success of our very special guest who is sitting close by me. Not only has she broken all records in music sales, LPs, discs, and tapes, but I've just clinched a five-million-dollar deal that will take her on an extensive European tour which includes the United Kingdom! Ladies and gentlemen, charge your glasses and please be upstanding. I want you to join with me in drinking a toast to the continued success of our very own lovely Velana Domingo."

The crowd proudly cheered and held their glasses high. "Velana." The name was chanted round the room; a rapturous burst of applause broke out. Guida and Collette were the first to shake Velana's hand and congratulate her. She was astounded and totally devoid of speech at that moment. A European tour! And of the United Kingdom! It had been surprise enough when she had won the audition in Olhão – she still had to pinch herself about that – but never, never, had she ever dreamed that it would lead to this!

"I told you, the world's your oyster," Guida said, her own face all pink and sparkly with exuberance. "Nothing can stop you now, Velana, and we'll be with you every step of the way."

"It might be a good idea to let your mother know," Collette said in her practical way. "I'll see to it as soon as I can."

"Oh, yes, Mamma." In the excitement of the last few minutes Velana had completely forgotten all about her mother and a stain of shame spread over her face. "Perhaps I could pay her a quick visit. I could be there and back in a day."

"The tour starts the day after tomorrow," Carlos Santos put in quickly, "which means you will all be leaving for London first thing in the morning.

That is why I arranged accommodation for you here. Your luggage has been collected from your hotel and placed in your bedrooms. I'll fill Collette in with all the details later but for now, have a nice lunch and enjoy yourselves." He glanced at Velana's anxious face. "It's the chance of a lifetime, my dear girl, you mustn't let anything stand in your way. Your mamma will be fine, Collette will let her know what's happening, I'm sure she will understand and be delighted for you." He moved away to mingle with the rest of the guests.

"He's right, you know," Collette told Velana. "This is a wonderful opportunity for you to expand your horizons. I used to worry about being away from my family for any length of time until I discovered they had accepted having a roving daughter and were happily getting on with their own lives."

Velana bit her lip. "I know, I'm just being a baby; Mamma and I were always very close and it's taking me a while to get used to being away from her all the time." She brightened. "I'm glad I took English at school. It's going to come in really useful. I can speak it fairly fluently and used to practise with my friend Jose who also took it. We used to help each other with all our school work."

"Who is Jose?" Guida asked curiously. "I don't think we met him when we were in Olhão."

"No, you never met him, he's a wonderful person and is in Paris just now training to become a priest."

Guida noticed the way Velana's eyes lit up when she mentioned Jose's name and she took the younger girl's hand and squeezed it tightly. "It's the experiences in life that mould us into what we are and what we can be," she said quietly. "You've got most of yours in front of you yet, and because you concern yourself so much with what other people are feeling you'll never become spoiled or bigheaded."

Velana stared out of the window. She could see in the distance, standing proud on top of the hill, the statue of Cristo Rei overlooking the city of Lisbon, as if casting a continuous blessing on all its inhabitants.

She wondered what Jose was doing at this very moment and what he'd be thinking about her success. She had written in answer to his letter, letting him know what had been happening to her, and she knew he would be proud of her and would be praying for her wherever she was.

Chapter Thirteen

The flight to London ran smoothly, apart from the take-off. It was the first time that Velana had flown and she felt her stomach lurching as the plane climbed steeply out of Lisbon airport. It was like going up in an endless lift at speed, ever upwards into the blue sky, leaving the earth far behind till all she could see were matchbox houses and cars that looked like toys crawling along winding ribbons that were roads. And then higher still, up through the clouds, with the view gradually disappearing. But it wasn't long before the plane levelled off and she could feel herself relaxing enough to take an interest in what was going on inside the cabin.

There was no rest for Collette and Guida during the flight, they were kept busy dealing with all the advertising paperwork for the tour, which was pretty extensive as they were doing all the major cities in the UK, starting in London and working their way up north to Scotland. Guida was also working with her music chart, doing some arrangements to suit Velana's terrific voice range, the fame of which was now sweeping across Europe and the world.

Velana sat back and thought about the life she had known at home in the farmlands of southern Portugal. It all seemed so far away now, so out of reach, yet she knew she would always want to go back there, it was a part of her life that she could never forget, no matter how far she travelled, or how many new experiences she might have . . .

She felt her eyes growing heavy. She hadn't been able to sleep much last night even though she'd stayed up late. It had been hectic since early morning and it was nice to be still for a while – even though she was in a Boeing thousands of feet up in the heavens.

As they flew into London airport Velana blessed herself and let out a great sigh of relief as the wheels touched down on the tarmac.

It was while they were taxiing along the runway that Guida gasped and pointed to where a contingent of fans were lining the airport building, chanting "Velana, Velana".

Collette's hand flew to her mouth and she gave a little laugh. "The news has travelled fast. What do you think of that, Miss Domingo? Your public can't wait to greet you."

Velana couldn't answer. All she could do was to stare out of wide blue eyes at the waving hands and scarves flying like banners to welcome her to Britain.

Guida and Collette hustled her off the plane as quickly as they could but as they came through customs a crowd of eager fans pushed forward, shouting for Velana's autograph, surrounding her closely and making her feel scared and hardly able to get her breath.

Then suddenly, through the mêlée, there came a voice, that of a tall young man who was standing in front of her with camera gear strapped to his shoulders.

"Come on," he yelled in a clear, deep Scottish accent, "hold on to my straps and I'll lead you out of this little lot."

Guida and Collette and the rest of the party had been separated from her in the crowd and had disappeared from view. Frantically Velana looked for them but the man was speaking again, urging her to vacate the scene and she took hold of his straps and held onto them grimly as he pushed his way through the masses, repeating over and over, "Gangway please, BBC. Out of the way now."

Soon they were outside the airport, hurrying along to the car park where he opened the door of a large van and helped Velana get in.

"What about the rest of the party?" she asked in concerned tones.

"Oh, they'll be along shortly, don't worry about them, they've probably had to deal with this kind of thing before. The main thing is to get you to your hotel safely and we'll take it from there."

He gave the driver instructions. Soon they were motoring towards the city of London and then he settled himself back in his seat and introduced himself. "I'm Hamish MacSween and I work for the BBC. We're doing a documentary about you and will be touring with you on the road so you'll be stuck with us I'm afraid."

He took her hand and shook it firmly and although he was a complete stranger Velana felt a strange attraction to him. He was tall and handsome with piercing blue eyes and fair hair and when he smiled it lit up his whole face.

"Welcome to London," he said with a grin. "It isn't everyone who gets a reception quite as lively. It must have been nerve-wracking for you back there."

"I'm starting to get used to big crowds but that was something else and really a bit scary," Velana agreed as she straightened her dress which had actually been slightly torn in the crush.

"Don't worry about your clothes, you can get cleaned

up at the hotel; the driver has radioed ahead and contacted security so everything will be OK, and I'll keep my eye on things. It's the price you pay for fame, as no doubt you've been told already. You've become a household name here in Britain, everyone's raving about you. They adore you and love your songs and I must say I'm one of your biggest fans." He gazed at her thoughtfully. "There's something haunting about your voice, it sort of tears at the heartstrings. I feel I almost know what you're thinking when you sing."

Velana felt herself warming towards Hamish MacSween. She liked the happy way he smiled, the honesty in his open face, the boyish enthusiasm in his manner. It was as if she had known him for a long time and she felt quite relaxed sitting beside him.

"Are you from Scotland?" she asked a little hesitantly. "Your accent is so different from anything I've heard before. Also, your name – MacSween. Someone once told me that Scottish people all have names beginning with 'Mac'."

"Not quite," he laughed. "But you're right, I am Scottish and proud of it."

"Which part of the country do you come from?"

"The Western Isles," he said, unable to keep a note of pride from his voice. "An island called Layish. My family still live there. My father is the local minister."

"Have you ever heard of an island called Corrish?" As she asked the question she held her breath as she waited for his answer.

He stared at her in surprise. "Yes, I do as a matter of fact, how odd that you should ask. It's one of the neighbouring islands off Layish; the western seaboard is dotted with hundreds of them, every shape, size and description. I've travelled to quite a few corners of the globe but to me the Hebridean islands of Scotland are the most beautiful in the world. When the evening sky is aflame with the setting sun they're like a jewelled necklace, purple and blue and green, scattered across tranquil seas that have to be seen to be believed."

"Oh, what beautiful words!" Velana cried. "The way you describe them makes me feel as if I can see them. It must be a truly lovely place."

"It is," he said dreamily, "it truly is . . ."

His voice faded away and both of them sat silently for a moment, he thinking of his Hebridean home, she about the man who was her flesh and blood father, living on one of those wonderful islands that Hamish had just described. Hamish MacSween. How strange that fate had brought him to her, out of thousands of people, as if it was all part of a pattern, something that was meant to be.

Impulsively she took his hand and held it tightly and he responded by looking straight into her eyes and saying softly, "Would you like us to have dinner together tonight?"

"I'd love to," she said at once. "In fact, I'd be more than happy if you would be my escort from now on."

"It would be an honour, Velana." Still holding her eyes with his he raised her hand to his lips and kissed it gently. It was such a sweet and romantic gesture; she felt as if something inside her was going to melt and so entranced was she by the interlude that she jumped with fright when the driver called out in a big, bold cockney voice, "Hilton Hotel! And from the look of it, there's another welcoming committee waiting to meet you, Miss Domingo."

He brought the van to a halt at the hotel entrance and a small crowd of people came surging forward, peering in the tinted windows, trying to see if Velana was inside, rocking the van on its wheels in a most alarming manner.

"Quick, before they know you're in here." Hamish pushed a bundle into her hand. "Put this cap and jacket on and then no one will recognise you, they'll think you are one of the cameramen."

He strapped a couple of cameras onto Velana's shoulder as he was speaking and then directed her to follow him. Jumping out of the van he shouted, "Make way for the camera crew," and with Velana at his side he went quickly into the hotel.

"This is a wonderful disguise," she said as she removed the cap, letting her beautiful blonde hair cascade over her shoulders. The desk clerk saw her removing the cap and jacket and his jaw dropped open.

"Velana Domingo," Hamish introduced her proudly. "And the rest of the party will be along shortly once they get through the madding crowd." As if on cue, Guida and Collette came hurriedly in through the swing doors, looking harrassed and crumpled; Guida's skirt had been torn, her once immaculate jacket was now minus a sleeve, somebody had spilled Coca Cola on Collette's coat and she had lost a shoe during the crush at the airport.

"We should get danger money for this," Guida grumbled, pushing a strand of dark hair out of her eyes while Collette hobbled over to the desk to lean on it while she rubbed the sole of her foot.

They were a sorrowful sight to behold but the funny side of the whole episode struck Velana and she simply couldn't stop the bubbles of laughter rising in her throat. Guida and Collette glared at her, then they began to laugh too as anxiety changed to relief that they were all safe and sound inside the building and relatively all in one piece.

"We were really worried about you back there," Guida said at last. "We simply couldn't get near you and just kept getting pushed further and further away from you."

"I was frightened too," Velana admitted, "until I was rescued by a knight in shining cameras. Let me introduce you to Hamish MacSween, the man who rescued me. Hamish, this is Guida and Collette, my musical and technical advisers."

"Pleased to meet you." Hamish shook them warmly by the hand. "You'll be seeing a lot of me in the next few months; I'm with the BBC and we're doing a film about your tour – but don't worry—" His smile flashed out. "We aren't filming just now – we'll wait till you get cleaned up first."

"Thanks for that small crumb of comfort," Guida said dryly while Collette removed her remaining shoe and put it into the nearest waste bin with a wry expression on her face.

They checked in at the desk and then the hotel manager escorted them to the lift, trying politely not to look too much at Guida's missing sleeve and Collette's shoeless feet.

Hamish whispered to Velana, "I'll see you later then, how about seven-thirty? In the lobby. We can have a drink at the bar before dinner."

"Sounds wonderful." Despite her recent ordeal Velana looked radiant as the lift doors closed and they vanished out of sight.

Chapter Fourteen

Garlands of flowers came showering onto the stage of the Albert Hall as Velana ended her show to the rapturous applause of a packed house. She smiled, blew kisses, and bowed at the audience who were giving her a standing ovation, then she turned and indicated her appreciation of Guida who was conducting the orchestra.

Cheering and whistling broke out, the entire orchestra stood up and they too began applauding; it was truly a moving and wonderful moment for Velana and tears sprang to her eyes when she saw Hamish in the wings with his camera, giving her the thumbs up sign and laughing with the joy of the occasion.

A glow of warmth spread through her being. She felt like this every time she was near him and when he looked at her.

She had gone out to dinner with him a couple of times since meeting him and each time she felt closer to him. He was so charming and warm, he knew how to treat a lady; he complimented her on her appearance and made her feel special, and every time they kissed goodnight he was very gentle, though she sensed the passions rising within him.

She, too, held herself back. Jose was still pulling at her heartstrings; she couldn't forget how it had been with him and she felt it was too soon to allow herself to be loved by another man.

Even so, she couldn't help but think of Hamish in an intimate way; he was a very attractive man, one who had begun to infiltrate the defences she had built around her heart, no matter how hard she tried to push him away.

After the show they all piled into a taxi to go back to the hotel, everyone talking at once about the success and excitement of the evening, Velana, Guida and Collette sitting in the back, Hamish in the front beside the driver.

"Oh, my bag!" Velana exclaimed as they drove up to the hotel entrance. "I must have left it in the dressing room at the theatre. I'll have to go back for it, all my things are in it. You can all go in, you needn't worry about me, I won't be long."

"I'll come with you," Hamish decided promptly, jumping into the back seat beside her as soon as Guida and Collette got out. He gave instructions to the driver and the taxi moved away, leaving the two women on the pavement looking rather bemused as they stood watching it go.

An odd little silence sprung up between Hamish and Velana as they sped through the night. She was very aware of his presence beside her, she could feel the warmth of his thigh next to hers, could sense his tension as he moved about in his seat, as if he couldn't wait for the taxi to stop so that he could get out and rid himself of his restlessness.

He turned his head to look at her and in the half-darkness she could see the pleading in his eyes, the tautness on his face, as if he was mutely appealing to her to understand how he was feeling.

Taking his hand she gave it a little squeeze but still neither of them spoke and both of them were relieved when the driver drew up at their destination and they could at last get out of the vehicle.

The night watchman was the only one left at the stage door when they arrived and he raised his eyebrows enquiringly when he saw them coming towards him.

"I just want to pick up my purse," Velana explained. "I must have left it here since I can't seem to find it anywhere else."

"That's all right, Miss Domingo," the man said respectfully. "Just pull the door shut when you leave, I'm going into the office to watch 'Come Dancing' on the telly."

Everything was very quiet inside the theatre, so different from the noise, bustle, and excitement earlier in the evening. It was also a bit creepy and Hamish took her hand as they made their way along the dark corridors to the dressing room.

Almost immediately Velana spotted her purse lying on the dressing table and gladly she rushed forward to pick it up. As she turned, Hamish took her into his arms and before she could say anything he was kissing her passionately and murmuring against her lips, "I've fallen in love with you, Velana; I can't think of anything else but you. I always thought I was in control of my life but you've changed all that. Please, please, say you love me a little bit in return."

For answer she took his face in her hands and tenderly kissed his eyes, his nose, his mouth. "Lock the door," she whispered into his ear. "I think we deserve a few moments alone together – so that I can show you that I love you too."

He did as she bade him. "There, we're locked in," he said, giving the door an extra rattle to make sure. He turned to look at her and with a laugh he added, "You didn't arrange all this did you? It all seems a bit too good to be true."

"Of course I didn't." Her eyes sparkled. "I'm just a

naïve country girl, remember, such a thought would never enter my head. But don't let's waste time talking. I want you to come here, Hamish MacSween, I need you very, very much at this moment."

They fell into one another's arms, both of them hungry for the kisses that came one upon the other, undressing each other even as their mouths met over and over, till at last they were standing naked together. Wordlessly he scooped her up in his strong arms and laid her down on the couch in the corner of the room.

Kneeling down beside her he began to kiss her again, tenderly at first, then, feeling her respond to him, his mouth became harder and fiercer and more demanding.

"You're so beautiful," he told her, drinking in every detail of her curvaceous young body, gently stroking her breasts as he spoke, feathering her erect rosy nipples with his fingertips, kissing them with his warm lips, his mouth travelling down till it reached her belly, his tongue running in fiery circles round her navel.

The sweet, hot fire of her aroused passions ran through her in waves and she knew now how parched she had been from the lack of being loved by a man. It was like a volcano erupting inside her. She spoke to him in a confused string of husky, mumbling words, her lips hard against his as he took her with him to the heights of unbearable desire.

And when they could both wait no longer for the ultimate expression of their love she clung to him as he entered her body, meeting his demands with hers, kissing his burning mouth as spasms of almost unbearable pleasure tore at her quivering body till the blinding golden light of their mutual fulfilment burst triumphantly into its delirious peak. "My sweet

Velana," Hamish gasped. "I think you're the most perfect creature in the whole wide world."

She pressed her warm lips against his face and kissed him with all the love and tenderness in her heart. Her skin was glowing from the fire of their lovemaking; she felt a deep and wonderful contentment flowing through her being and lifting one finger she lazily traced the outline of his mouth.

"Sweet, darling, Hamish," she murmured. "You make me feel so alive and vibrant; I wish I could sing out our love across the rooftops. Have I known you in another time, I wonder? I feel somehow as if we've always belonged together."

"I feel the same way," he told her huskily. "I've never, ever known anyone like you. I want you to lie with me always and be forever in my heart."

They lay in each other's arms for a long time, then suddenly he propped himself on one elbow and gazing down at her he said laughingly, "Tell me, I have to know, did you really forget your purse tonight?"

She gazed back at him, her blue eyes large and unwavering when she replied seriously, "Of course I did. At least – I remembered to forget where it was, when I left the theatre."

They stared at one another then they collapsed laughing together in total joyous abandonment.

Chapter Fifteen

The weeks and months that followed were a sensual odyssey for Velana and Hamish. Whenever they could they made love, feeling that they couldn't get enough of each other. But it was more than physical pleasures that delighted and thrilled them, it was all the shared happy experiences that they cherished more than anything, like meeting after her shows and walking under the stars in the moonlight, waking up and greeting each new day together.

They were in love and that made everything right and good. Time seemed to fly past on golden wings whenever they met and they were never at a loss for things to talk about. Over dinner, at favourite hotels and restaurants of whatever city they happened to be in, they had long conversations and were both totally attuned to what the other was thinking and feeling.

Their discussions were very profound; they confided everything about themselves and their past and she was startled by the fact that though their outward circumstances had been different, their lives had developed along the same parallel lines.

Guida and Collette were happy that she had found love. She looked so radiant and shone like a star; even her voice sounded better, if that was possible. She sang with the feeling of a woman in love. Her singles, tapes, and CD sales, rocketed all over Europe.

It meant a lot of hard work for her and by popular demand she was obliged to work on a tight schedule, but Hamish was always by her side, supporting her and helping her with any problems that might arise.

She felt well and fit and very, very happy but never forgot her home in Olhão. She kept in constant touch with her mother and sent gifts of money, actions that Theresa objected to fiercely though she was somewhat mollified when she realised that she could use them to enhance the quality of a life that was often lonely for her. Communication with her daughter had been her biggest drawback and one of the first things she did was to have a telephone installed in the farmhouse, an innovation that delighted her, as now she could keep in touch with Velana, no matter where in the world she might happen to be.

It was no surprise to either Hamish or Velana when she discovered she was going to have his baby. They were both over the moon with happiness and when she told him the news he picked her up off her feet and danced with her all round the room.

"This makes our lives complete," he laughed joyfully, kissing the tip of her nose as he came to a breathless halt and collapsed with her on the couch.

"Should I tell Mamma?" she wondered aloud. "It might come as a bit of a shock to her. She doesn't even know about you yet."

He thought for a few moments before saying, "Better tell her about me first; later you can tell her about the baby – or keep us both a secret till the time comes and in that way she can have all the surprises together."

"I'll have a think about it," Velana decided. "She has a right to know everything but I'll give myself a few days to get used to the idea of becoming a mother before letting anyone know. For now, it'll be our secret, just yours and mine, my darling, dearest man."

Some days later, Theresa was both stunned and delighted when she heard the news over the phone. "A baby," she repeated breathlessly. "I can't believe it, you're only a baby yourself yet, but there is nothing that will make you a woman quicker than a child of your own. I didn't even know you were married but then, girls these days do everything in a rush."

"I'm not married, Mamma," Velana said quietly. "Hamish and I – well – we never even discussed that, but we love each other very much and that's all that seems to matter at the moment."

"Not married?" There was a long pause then Theresa said slowly, "Who am I to judge? At least, you have the father of your child there by your side; I didn't, and I suffered for it until your Papa Mario came along and took me under his wing."

"Oh, Mamma." Tears caught in Velana's throat. "It must have been terrible for you, but you're right, I have Hamish. He's a wonderful man and I hope you'll get to meet him before very long."

"I hope so too, him and the baby. You'll have to take time off now, Velana, you must rest and eat plenty of fruit and vegetables."

"I know, Mamma," Velana laughed. "Don't worry about me and I'll be in touch again as soon as I can."

Both Guida and Collette were at first rather taken aback by her news but very soon they came to terms with it and even began to be quite excited by the prospect.

"There will come a point when you'll definitely have to take it easier," Collette soon decided. "We can't have you going on stage looking like a Christmas pudding when all your fans have come to expect a beautiful blonde nymph with not an ounce of fat in sight."

They all laughed at this but Velana knew that Collette was right. She would have to ease off on the live concerts, though Guida said she could keep on recording, her voice was at its best just now. So far she had been able to sail through rehearsals and could record perfectly after only one or two takes.

Meanwhile, she went on as before, the two older women always trying to make sure that she never overstrained herself, Guida in particular being very aware of her responsibilities. She loved Velana like a sister, everything that they did revolved around her, she was the important one. But Guida underestimated herself. When she and Velana performed together on stage they were a perfect duo, with an aura of power about them that influenced everything and everyone around them, bonding the orchestra, the team, and themselves into a tightly integrated group with intense concentration and total dedication.

It was that powerful dedication that frightened Hamish a little. It was a way of life that he didn't truly understand and in which he felt he had no part. Velana's frightening apprehension before a show, the electric tension as she waited backstage before she went on, the chanting and clapping of thirty-thousand fans roaring their approval when the blinding laser lights lit up the broad stage and she began to sing.

How, he often asked himself, could he compete with thirty-thousand adoring fans? The thought of it made him feel quite small. Where was his place in all this? Velana had told him how isolated she herself sometimes felt on stage and how precious to her were the warm, wonderful intimate hours they shared together. He wanted desperately to believe that, he loved her dearly and wanted to take care of her and always to be with her.

His chance of having her more to himself came some weeks before she was due to give birth, it having been discovered that she was expecting not one but two babies. The thought of twins disconcerted them both at first but they very quickly came to terms with it and joyfully hugged one another in their excitement.

With some well-earned time on her hands, Guida took the opportunity to fly home to be with her parents for a while, coming back refreshed and ready to face anything. With her striking good looks she was never short of dates and frequently went out on the town to enjoy herself.

Collette on the other hand seemed perfectly content to be around Velana and Hamish; she had begun to look upon them as her family and was always to hand if she was needed for anything.

"Wouldn't you like to get married and have children of your own?" Velana asked her once, to which Collette had replied that she was quite happy the way she was, she had all the family she needed right here beside her, and another back home in Oporto that she could visit whenever she felt like it.

"What more could anybody want?" she had said lightly. "I'm luckier than some and better off than most."

"But you can't be on the road forever," Velana had persisted. "You'll surely want to have a home of your own someday."

"What good would I be with a home of my own?" Collette had laughed. "I've been so used to having everything done for me I'd make a useless housewife and would burn and break everything I touched."

After that Velana hadn't pursued the subject; she

liked having Guida and Collette around her, they were both enthusiastically looking forward to being aunts to her children and it was lovely to go shopping with them for all the little things that the babies would need when they came along.

Chapter Sixteen

Because she was expecting twins, Velana had been taken into hospital a few days before the babies were due. After two false alarms she went into labour in earnest and Hamish paced up and down outside the delivery room, listening to her cries, feeling some of her pain, wondering how he could have put her through all this agony and vowing that it would never happen again.

After an anxiety-laden wait that seemed to last forever, a baby's high-pitched cry echoed through the room, followed by another fifteen minutes later.

The sister in charge came bustling out to where Hamish was standing, staring out of the window and biting his nails.

"You've got two lovely babies, Mr MacSween," she told him, "so stop biting your nails and come and see your son and daughter."

Hamish took a deep breath. He hadn't eaten or slept in more than twenty-four hours and now that the waiting was over, a flood of relief replaced the anxiety in his belly, making him feel suddenly weak. The last thing he remembered was walking towards Velana's bed. That was when his legs turned to jelly, his head started to spin, and he passed out on the delivery room floor.

One of the young nurses cried, "Mr MacSween!" and ran to his aid but the sister said hard-heartedly,

"Oh leave him be, he's just fainted; he can't fall any farther than the floor and no doubt he'll come round in a moment or two. I need your help with the mother and babies."

"Oh, but you have to help him," Velana cried out, "he's a big part of all this and I want him to see his children."

"Oh, all right." The sister relented as she tidied the bed, leaving the little nurse to help Hamish onto a chair at the bedside and give him a drink of water.

Hamish sipped the water, shook his head in an effort to clear it, then he gazed across at Velana and said sheepishly, "Trust me to make a fool of myself. I'm sorry, sweetheart, I don't know what came over me, it must have been nerves or something."

"Stop worrying," Velana told him softly, a smile lighting her face. "Just look at what we've made between us – Edward, our son, and Eva, our lovely little daughter."

Hamish stared at the two babies lying cocooned in Velana's arms. "They're like a couple of wrinkled pink peaches," he said with a grin, "but they're beautiful for all that and I like the names you've chosen for them."

With his finger he gently stroked the soft cheeks of his children then turning to Velana he gazed at her tenderly. She had come through the ordeal of labour well; there was a sparkle of colour in her face though her eyes were tired, with blue shadows underneath.

"Thank you, my darling," he said huskily, "for making our love so complete."

Leaning over, he nuzzled her lips with his, only to be boxed in the face by a tiny fist waving in the air. The new parents giggled and held onto one another for precious long moments before the door opened to admit Guida and Collette, bearing large bouquets of flowers.

There followed several minutes of confusion when everybody hugged and congratulated one another, then it was the turn of the twins to come under scrutiny. A mist of tears shone in Guida's eyes when she beheld the tiny faces.

"Excuse me, please," she sniffed, hastily dabbing her eyes. "I'm a hard-bitten businesswoman as a rule but babies have always done this to me; I have no earthly idea why because I don't intend to have any for years yet, if at all. It's just, they're so new and innocent and trusting . . . Oh, stop it!" she scolded herself with a laugh and turning her attention to Velana she continued, "I'm so happy for you, you look wonderful lying there – motherhood really suits you."

Collette, who had excused herself and gone outside, came back to say. "I've taken the liberty of calling your mother in Portugal, Velana; she's on the line waiting to speak to you now."

A nurse wheeled in the trolley phone and handed Velana the receiver while Guida and Collette each took a baby into their arms and walked with them round the room.

"Hello, Mamma," Velana said a little nervously. "I've just made you a grandmamma twice over. The babies are lovely, they're called Edward and Eva and you'll be so proud when you see them . . ."

As she was speaking she was holding in her hand the two little prayer books that Jose and Father Silvas had given her. She always drew strength from them every time she touched and read them. She kept them near her at all times, together in their little box, remembering Jose whenever she looked at the bright red poppy petals pressed into pages that still showed the traces of her tears, and finding humour and comfort in the words that Father Silvas had written: *'Be good sweet maid and let who will be clever'*.

She had often wondered, since leaving Portugal, if she had been as good as the old priest would have liked but she knew that he would understand anyway; he had always been a person of great wisdom and strength, just two of the reasons why his parishioners had always loved him so much.

Theresa spoke for a while on the phone, then Maria – who happened to be visiting the Domingo farm at the time – came on, full of lavish blessings and chatter and little chuckles of happiness.

When Theresa returned to the line, Velana said, "Mamma, I'd like you to speak to Hamish, the father of your grandchildren. I think it is time you two got to know one another."

Hamish took the phone. "Hello Mamma Theresa. I hope you don't mind me calling you that; it sounds a bit holy I know, but the way Velana talks about you makes you sound almost saint-like, which worries me sometimes as I don't think I could ever be more than a very earthly human being with a lot of human faults."

A girlish giggle sounded on the other end of the line. Hamish was obviously an instant hit with Theresa. He could speak Portuguese fairly well by now and she had a smattering of English and they went on to converse in such an easy manner it was as if they had known one another for years.

"Don't worry about Velana," he told her, "I know you must miss her and fret about her, but I'm here to look after her and the babies."

The tone of his voice was so soothing it touched Theresa's heart to the core and quietly she began to sob and say, "God bless you, my son, I hope you can come and see us soon; all the people here love Velana and play her music at local functions every chance they get, it would be wonderful if you could come to Olhão."

"We'll do our very best to come and see you, Mamma Theresa, as soon as we possibly can." Hamish returned, a great affection for Velana's mother spreading through his veins. He had promised Velana that while they were in the north he would take her to Scotland to meet his parents, but that need only be for a short visit. Afterwards they could go to Portugal for a longer vacation, Mamma Theresa had waited well to see her daughter again and now she had her grandchildren to look forward to as well.

Hamish said his goodbyes and handed the phone back to Velana. "Take care, Mamma, and God bless," she said shakily. "We'll be home to see you as soon as we can; we need all the baby clothes we can get so if you like you can maybe start knitting things for when we arrive."

Her eyes were bright with tears when she put the receiver down. She was exhausted now and when the nurse came back she told everyone that it was time for them to go as the new mother was needing a well-earned rest. The babies were taken away to the nursery and Guida and Collette took their leave.

Hamish seized his opportunity and gathering Velana into his arms he kissed her long and deeply and murmured, "My wonderful sweetheart, I love you so much; you've made me so happy, I feel like shouting from the rooftops that I'm a daddy and that my lady is the most talented and gracious person in the whole wide world."

Velana's eyes were growing heavy but she held onto

him and whispered, "I've always loved that romantic heart of yours, Hamish MacSween, and I want you always to remember how much you mean to me – as my dearest love and as the father of my children."

Chapter Seventeen

Velana Domingo flies north for long vacation with new baby twins.

Those were the general headlines in all the national newspapers as Velana, Hamish, the twins, Guida and Collette, flew into Glasgow airport under a grey, wet, mid-morning sky.

The reporters and cameramen were already standing on the tarmac, waiting as the plane landed and taxied on the runway. But Hamish had planned the trip well ahead and had arranged for a helicopter to be standing by, and with one well-organised manoeuvre the party were transferred to it in a matter of minutes and whisked off into the western sky, leaving Glasgow airport and the foiled media behind.

They were heading for Layish, Hamish's island home, the place where he had been brought up under the shadow of the strict laws of the church, forced on him by his father who was the local minister. Ever since Hamish could remember, Sunday had been a day of worship, with church services, bible readings, and prayer meetings, taking precedence above all else. Everything he had done had revolved round the Sabbath day; he hadn't been allowed to play football or games of any kind, he couldn't even fly a kite on a Sunday because it was considered to be irreverent.

But he wasn't the only one who'd had to adhere to

the rules. The islanders didn't dare do a washing or hang their clothes out; they weren't supposed to fix fences, repair walls, or indulge in manual labour of any sort; even the playing fields and swing parks were chained up and the island cockerels confined to barns, sheds, and under peat creels in case they should cast lustful beady eyes upon the flirtatious hens in their society.

In his teenage years, Hamish had started to rebel against his father and the church. He began to flaunt the Sabbath rulings – he played football, flew his kite and roamed his beloved island beaches, delighting in the sight and sound of the wild Atlantic waves crashing on the rocks, revelling in the sense of freedom that he felt.

He had yearned to escape from his father's gloomy shadow and when he finally left the island for his college education his euphoria knew no bounds. But the pull of the Hebrides never left his heart and he had returned regularly, albeit for brief visits, and then only to see his mother. Anything longer brought all the old frustrations flooding back, made him want to shake his father and tell him to stop acting like a god and start behaving like a man.

Now he was going back to Layish, this time with his very own little family, and he hoped with all his heart that his father would welcome them and see just what a happy man he could be if he allowed his eyes to open to all that was good and precious in life . . .

Velana, snuggled up beside him with baby Eva in her arms, nudged him out of his thoughts and asked how much farther they had to go. For answer, he put his arm round her shoulder and pulled her head down beside his so that they were looking together out of the window as the helicopter banked slightly and flew over a mainland peninsula before heading out to sea. The cloudy mist cleared into a beautiful blue sky and on the horizon they could see little dots that were islands in the distance.

"Won't be long now," said Hamish excitedly, "maybe another fifteen to twenty minutes. Oh, wait, over yonder, there's your island! Corrish! It's easy to spot with its triple peaks towering into the sky."

Velana felt a thrill of excitement rushing through her, making the hairs on the back of her neck stand up as she surveyed Corrish far below. It looked a wondrous place with its lush green terrain and its lofty pinnacles seeming to rise straight up out of the sea.

She felt as if she could touch them as they passed over the island and she wondered if the man who was her real father was still alive and living down there somewhere.

She hadn't told Hamish about him, all he knew was that she had family connections on the island and she had left it at that, though she had promised herself that she would visit Corrish as soon as it was possible for her to do so. She wanted to meet Ian McKinnon; she wanted to look upon the face of the man who had loved and left her mother all those years ago.

But just now the children were demanding some attention, baby Edward was wriggling and crying in Guida's arms and she cradled him and sang a little lullaby as Collette took two bottles of milk out of the thermos box and placed one of the teats between his little cushion lips. He locked onto it and gobbled away hungrily while Velana took the other bottle and fed his small sister.

All was quiet now but for the sound of the helicopter zooming over the tops of the dotted islands, then the pilot called out, "Look out everybody, Layish dead ahead."

As the helicopter began to lose height Guida observed that the island was much flatter than the others they had passed.

"That's right," agreed the pilot, "it's like a large carpet floating on the sea and because of that it's much easier to land on."

"How big is it?" asked Collette, staring down at the oblong of green below.

"Six miles long by three and a half miles wide," Hamish supplied with a quiver of excitement in his voice. "Look, there's the church and the manse standing on a knoll above the village."

The pilot banked left to fly over the rooftops, hovering close to the church steeple for a moment before dropping down to land on the village green in front of the church.

Some of the villagers ran up to help the visitors disembark and unload the luggage as the rotor blades slowly halted and the noise of the engine stopped, and then all was quiet but for the sound of the wind blowing in from the sea.

Velana had no time to take in much of anything, her first impression being that of the minister's dark figure emerging out of the lych-gate of the churchyard and walking down towards the helicopter.

"Well, hello my boy, how are you?" was the Revd MacSween's greeting to his son as he approached.

"Hello, Father," returned Hamish politely. Drawing Velana close to him he introduced her and the others and then he indicated the babies. "These are your grandchildren, Eva and Edward, seasoned travellers already and hardly a peep out of them on the journey."

The minister glanced at them. "Hmm, fancy names, but have you given them the other one yet?"

Hamish frowned in puzzlement.

"MacSween, lad, MacSween. It would be good idea to do the proper thing by them and get married. You don't want them growing up believing that values aren't important anymore."

Hamish clenched his fists. It was starting, already it was starting, but in the next moment his father's tone changed and he spoke quite jovially as he led the way up the path towards the manse.

"Come away in all of you, Mother has lunch all ready. I'm sure you must be ready for it."

Velana looked at him. He was a tall man with a slight stoop and grey hair combed to one side to cover a bald patch. His piercing dark eyes looked out from under beetling brows, he had a large nose and lantern jaws and a deep commanding voice that made people sit up and listen.

As they entered the hallway, Hamish's mother came out to meet them. She was tall and thin with pleasant features and fair hair fading to white; she carried herself very erect and altogether her appearance was gracious and ladylike. Velana thought that Hamish looked like her, he certainly wasn't a bit like his father, except for his height.

"I'm very pleased to meet you, Mrs McSween." Velana extended her hand and it was taken and shaken warmly. "I've heard so much about you and it's so lovely to be here at last."

"Oh, do call me Maud," Mrs McSween said in a voice that was slightly shaky. "You must be Guida and Collette," she went on, turning to them. "I must say I'm most delighted to meet you all and . . ." She broke off to stare at the babies. "They're beautiful," she said quietly. "Can I hold them? Just for a moment? It's been so long . . ."

The twins were placed in her arms. "Your grandchildren," Velana said proudly and Maud stood there in the hallway, holding the babies and rocking them gently, tears of joy trickling down her cheeks.

Hamish was clicking away with his camera as everyone was introduced, making sure he got his mother smiling down at her grandchildren with love and pride in her eyes.

Afterwards she led the way into the dining room and they had no sooner seated themselves round the table than the minister's booming voice echoed round the room. "For what we are about to receive may the Lord make us truly thankful . . ." He went on, saying the words mournfully and solemnly, while everyone sat around in silence, heads bowed, not daring to move a muscle.

"Amen." Hamish said the word hurriedly as his father ended the long monologue, which would have been much more effective had he kept it short and simple.

Maud plunged a ladle into a steaming cauldron of lentil soup; plates were passed round.

"Smells wonderful," Guida commented appreciatively.

"Dig in then," Maud instructed, her face flushed and happy-looking.

Everybody dug in and a busy clatter filled the room.

"Lovely food, Maud," Collette said as roast beef was followed by home-made apple pie piped over with creamy custard.

"Plain but good," nodded Maud.

Hamish looked at her affectionately. "Mother was always too modest for her own good. She's a great cook, one of the reasons I always keep coming home."

There was a short silence, the minister coughed and ended the meal with a mercifully quick prayer of thanks and Maud took the visitors up the dark creaky stairs to their rooms. It was an old house and a bit draughty but the bedrooms were small and cosy with attic windows that looked out over the bay.

In her own room, Velana placed the twins in the two small cradles that Maud had had specially built for them by one of the local fishermen, complete with little rockers so that the least bit of movement set them rhythmically swinging to and fro.

She looked out of the window and was quite moved by the beauty of the island and all the little islands beyond. On the distant horizon she could see the triple peaks of Corrish, merging between sea and sky in subtle blendings of blue and grey.

"Come and see the wonderful view," she called to Guida and Collette who were unpacking in the next room. As they came in she added, "Just looking at it makes me feel inspired to sing."

"You're on," Guida laughed. "I'll get the keyboard set up and maybe we could do some work while we're here."

"Wait till you've seen the white shell sand beaches and the light red rocks and the turquoise blue sea." Hamish came in at that moment and sat on the bed. "That will really give you something to sing about though you mustn't forget we aren't here to work."

"Point taken, and if we're to see all that we'd better finish unpacking," Collette decided and left the room with Guida at her heels.

Hamish put his arms around Velana and kissed her lovingly. "I'm so glad that we're all here together to enjoy the tranquillity of the island. Tomorrow, if you're good, I might take you over to the north bay to see the dolphins swimming just offshore; it's incredible watching them twisting and turning and performing acrobatics in the water. They really are very wise creatures and sometimes you can hear them communicating with each other."

Velana said, "That sounds wonderful," and in the same breath she added, "how long would it take us to sail to Corrish?"

"Oh, roughly a couple of hours. Maybe a bit more. I've never been there myself. When I was younger my father didn't encourage me to visit the other islands. As I told you before, he was very strict with me and used to keep tabs on me at all times. It was like being on a leash and when I grew up it became unbearable and I had to escape to see a bit of the world. But that's all in the past. Now I've got you and my little family to love and look after. You're my very own special and famous lady. I know I've got to share you with the rest of the world but as long as I can get a little part of you I'll be happy."

"Mmm, and I adore you too, Hamish MacSween," she murmured and buried herself deeper into his arms, feeling content to be here beside him in Layish, his boyhood home.

Chapter Eighteen

The days passed and the visitors had a wonderful time, roaming the island and discovering its tranquil atmosphere. "It's so peaceful," said Guida, "just the place to unwind." And Velana agreed with her that it was perfect for inspiration with the music of the wind and the sea all around.

Collette, on the other hand, loved to paint. She was a trained artist among all her other skills and whenever she could she set up her easel and canvas to try and capture some of the beautiful scenery. Although the locals were shy, a few of them were persuaded to model for her and she would sit for hours, sketching and painting them at work and at play around the little harbour bordering the village, where all types of boats sailed in to tie up for the night, sheltered from the strong westerly winds that blew in from the Atlantic Ocean.

Velana had made some enquiries as to when the ferry sailed for Corrish and the seaman she spoke to told her it called in every three days. She also asked him if he knew Ian McKinnon and did he still live on the island?

"Ay," nodded the man, "I know him well. He works a small croft on Corrish. He's a widower with three daughters; bonny girls they are too and a great help to their father."

When she heard this, Velana's heart skipped a beat. She had three half-sisters she hadn't known about and she vowed to herself she would go and visit them at the first opportunity. Having thus made up her mind she could hardly control herself as she sat down to dinner later that evening. Brimming over with excitement she told everyone that she planned to visit Corrish the very next day with the intention of looking up some relatives who lived on the island.

"Oh, and who would they be?" said the minister as he ladled soup into his bowl. "I might know them. I used to be minister on Corrish many years ago."

Velana took a deep breath and burst out, "Do you know a man called Ian McKinnon?"

"Y-es, I know of him," uttered the minister hesitantly. "What relation is he to you, may I ask?"

"He's my father," said Velana. "I've never ever met him and never even knew of his existence till my Papa Mario died and my mother told me about Ian McKinnon."

She had dropped a bombshell! The effect of her words on the minister was startling to say the least. His actions were frozen, and he sat, the soup ladle suspended in mid-air, his face a ghastly grey colour as he stared incredulously at Velana.

Maud's reaction to the news was also extreme. She had been leaning over the table, pouring potatoes from a heavy cast-iron pot onto a large plate, but as Velana's words took effect she swayed on her feet and the pot slipped from her grasp, smashing the plate to pieces.

Hamish instantly jumped up and caught his mother as she slumped backward onto a seat, muttering the words, "Mercy on us, mercy on us! How can this be? It's come back to haunt us! A twist of fate, a terrible twist of fate!" She began to sob uncontrollably and to cry out, "Oh, Lord! It was so wrong, but it's so long ago now! This can't be happening, please don't let it happen."

"What is it mother?" Hamish cried, his arms around her as he tried to console her. "What was wrong so long ago?"

Everybody was looking startled, not knowing what to make of the situation. A few moments ago they had been about to start their meal; everything had been normal, now this – Maud in a dreadfully distraught state, the minister ashen-faced and trembling.

It was he who spoke first. Looking straight at Hamish he said abruptly and with brutal frankness, "If what the girl says is true, and Ian McKinnon is indeed her father, then Velana Domingo, the mother of your children, is – by all that's unholy – your half-sister. You both have the same father."

"Stop this!" Hamish pleaded harshly. "You're my father . . ." His voice trailed away, he could say no more; he stared at the man in front of him with eyes that were dazed with shock.

"You might as well know now," the minister went on, "the truth is going to come out soon enough. It all happened many years ago. Your mother and I lived on Corrish. I was the minister of the church and we were involved in all the community projects. She did a bit of teaching and also took Gaelic evening classes for adults. That's how she came to meet and have an affair with the then fisherman, Ian McKinnon.

"Eventually she became pregnant and with you on the way we decided to leave the island for good and I was transferred here to Layish. You know the rest. I raised you as my own son. I know I was always a bit strict with you when you were child but it was the only way I knew how to teach you the laws of the Church, to fear God and resist temptation and sin."

As he was speaking, his dark piercing eyes had begun to bulge, his voice had grown louder, more commanding than ever, while Maud whimpered and cried in Hamish's arms.

"It was just something that happened. I was lonely when I did what I did," she moaned brokenly. "I never meant to hurt anyone, especially you, Hamish, the only child I was destined to have. You lit up my life, I lived only for you and gave you all the love I had in my heart."

But Hamish was in no fit state to comfort his mother any longer. Drawing away from her he gazed at her and shook his head. "I always thought there was no one like you, now . . ." His voice faded; blindly he stumbled out of the house, followed by Velana.

"Please, my darling, listen to me," she begged, "this needn't make any difference to us or the way we feel about each other. I don't care what anybody thinks. All that matters is you and me and the children. You will always be my love, I need you desperately to believe that."

But he hardly heard a word she said. Angrily he shook her hand from his arm and walked away from her, leaving her standing there in the manse garden, her eyes dry, though the tears were welling up inside her from the deep raw wound of her shattered heart.

Chapter Nineteen

Embarrassed beyond measure by the dreadful outcome of Velana's innocent desire to visit Corrish, Guida and Collette had gone upstairs, taking the twins with them. They could still hear the minister ranting and raving below, as if all the old resentments and hurt that had been eating away at him for years, had finally erupted.

He had never really forgiven his wife for her unfaithfulness but in an attempt to forget he had buried himself in his church work. Now it was all out in the open, the façade had crumbled, and he didn't care who suffered any more. The fragile feelings of Maud, the hurt bewilderment of Hamish, were the last considerations in the Revd MacSween's mind as he spilled out everything that had festered inside him for decades.

As one in a dream, Velana went slowly back into the house, her mind in a turmoil. It seemed so unbelievable that Hamish, her lover, the father of her children, was in actual fact, her blood kin.

The thought of it made her stomach churn and she jumped with fright when the minister suddenly came brushing past her, shouting, "I'm going to the church to ask that He might forgive us our sins. The only thing left now is prayer and meditation, everything else is finished!"

His booming voice echoed in Velana's ears, and she stood watching him go, his lantern jaws jutting, his stoop more pronounced than it had ever been.

The door slammed; only the tick of the grandfather clock in the hall and Maud's pitiful weeping, broke the silence. Velana felt very alone. She wondered how a person like MacSween could think of himself as a man of God. It seemed impossible that anyone could find comfort from him when he was so bitter about his own family life and so lacking in compassion. If he had thrashed it out with Maud at the beginning perhaps he would have been able to better cope with his feelings but he had locked it all away till everything that might once have been good in him had corroded and died.

Velana felt drained, so much so she was unable to go back into the kitchen to console Maud; instead she went up the rickety stairs to the bedroom where the twins were already tucked up in their cradles, sound asleep, Guida having just finished singing them a lullaby,

At Velana's entry she turned and said softly, "I'm so sorry for what happened down there. It was a terrible ordeal for you and Hamish to go through, his mother too. What will you do now?"

Velana sat down on the bed. "I'm more determined than ever to go and see the man who's at the root of all this unhappiness. In fact, I'm going tomorrow and I'm taking the twins with me."

"Let Collette and me come also," Guida said urgently. "I for one don't feel like hanging around here after all that's happened. Anyway, we promised your mother we would look after you, remember?"

Velana nodded. "You and Collette have been wonderful friends. I don't know what I'd have done without you and I'd like you both to be with me when I first set foot on Corrish. I don't think Hamish will want to come – he's totally devastated by all this. If he stays it might be a chance for him and his mother to talk everything over."

Sensing that Velana wanted to be alone for a while, Guida got up and went quietly to her own room to tell Collette about the plans to visit Corrish next day.

Velana sat at the window, listening to the gentle breathing of her sleeping babies. What would happen to them now, she wondered, if Hamish didn't want to be their father any more? She bit her lip and looked down at her tightly clenched hands, thinking how destiny had mapped out a very strange path for her to follow, allowing her to meet and fall in love with her half-brother. Now all their dreams were shattered and she didn't know how she was going to cope with the days that lay ahead.

She looked out of the window. The cascading light of the moon was shimmering over the vast reaches of the Atlantic Ocean and she could see the dark shapes of islands in the distance, like little ships anchored on the horizon. Something of the serenity of the scene found a small niche in her soul and she knelt down and said her prayers, thoughts of her mother, Jose, Father Silvas, and all her friends back home in Portugal, filling her mind as she did so.

The little car ferry chugged along on the crest of the waves before a following wind, its engines busily buzzing away below deck while above it the gulls hovered and screeched.

Collette had phoned ahead to the Corrish Hotel to ascertain that accommodation would be available if required. She had also hired a Range Rover from the local garage owner on Layish and she sat now in the driver's seat, the twins strapped into their carrycots in the back, the gentle rocking of the boat lulling them into a state of peaceful drowsiness.

Velana and Guida were at the bow, watching as Corrish came into view, its three peaks looking like giant fingers jutting out of the sea.

The ferry rounded a headland and sailed into a small natural harbour and Velana thought about Hamish and how he had been that morning when she had asked him if he would like to come over to Corrish with her.

He had looked at her, a dullness in his eyes that she had never seen before and a deadness in his voice when he'd said, "What, to see *him*? The cause of all this trouble? If you want to go you can, I'll just stay here, I've got a lot of thinking to do and I'll have to take care of Mother. I shouldn't blame her for what happened in the past, she must have been driven to do what she did out of despair and loneliness."

His voice had been solemn and gloomy. She had tried to comfort him but he hadn't responded. It was as if he had blanked her out of his thoughts, making her feel that she was in some way responsible for all this.

After that he had sat staring into space and didn't seem to care about anything any more and she had felt hurt and confused at his attitude. She knew he was building a wall between them and thought perhaps his strict upbringing might have something to do with the way he was behaving. She was at a loss to understand him but she knew one thing, she loved him dearly and always would, no matter what happened, nothing could change that . . .

The slight shuddering of the ferry's ramp being lowered brought Velana back from her thoughts. The village of Corrish came into view as Collette drove the Range Rover up the steep, cobbled slipway. The arrival of the ferry was obviously a highlight on the island.

Groups of people were standing about, watching the comings and goings of foot-passengers and vehicles; loaded fish boxes were being dragged onto the jetty by the local fishermen who were calling out loudly to each other in their native Gaelic tongue. The noise and the smell reminded Velana of her home in Olhão when, as a little girl, she would go down to the fish market with her mother to buy fresh sardines. She had loved the banter of the local people jabbering away to each other and now she felt the same about Corrish Harbour.

Collette drove on, up through the village with its shops and fishermen's cottages bordered by small, neat gardens. The scent of roses filled the air as Collette drew up at a crossroads where three roads led in different directions, and spying an old lady leaning on her garden gate Velana asked her if she knew where the McKinnon croft was.

The old lady's weather-beaten face opened up into a smile and she said in a lilting voice, "Take the road on the left for a couple of miles. The McKinnon croft is the first house you'll come to; don't go too fast in case you bump into the sheep on the way."

Velana thanked her and they moved off down the winding road, following the sea as they went. Here, the coastline was more rugged than on Layish, with some sheer cliff-faces dropping into the sea, interspersed with little coves connected by tidal caves that could be seen quite clearly from the road.

Despite her worries about Hamish, Velana could feel the excitement building up in her as they rounded a bend and a crofthouse came into view at the foot of the hill. It was a sturdy two-storey building, with white lime-washed walls and outhouses attached to the gable at the back. It was larger than Velana had imagined it to be, with fields running down from the hills, bordered by trees and stone walls leading right down to the beach and the water's edge.

"What a beautiful place!" exclaimed Guida. "It's like a Shangri-la, all on its own; everything looks so spic-and-span and orderly and obviously well cared for."

Collette drove the Range Rover almost to the front door of the croft and a black and white collie began to bark. Velana opened the passenger door to speak to it in a soothing voice and sensing her friendship it immediately started to wag its tail and lick her hand.

The door of the house opened. A well-proportioned girl came out on the step and called out in a clear island accent, "Bracken, leave the lady alone." She then turned her attention to Velana and said politely, "Hello, can I help you at all?"

"Yes, I was wondering, is this the McKinnon croft? If so, I'd like to speak to Mr McKinnon please."

She tried not to look as nervous as she felt, all the while asking herself if it had really been a good idea coming here. It might have been better to let sleeping dogs lie. If she hadn't mentioned Ian McKinnon to the Revd MacSween everything would still be as it was, the past would have remained buried, and she and Hamish would have remained blissfully ignorant and happy . . .

A tall, well-built man appeared behind the girl in the doorway and said in a warm, friendly voice, "I'm Mr McKinnon, is there something I can do for you?"

Velana stared at him and knew instinctively that this was her father. She drew in her breath and said, "Could I speak to you alone?"

"Yes, of course, let's go down the garden, I could do with a little stroll anyway."

Velana's heart was beating fast. The moment she had both dreaded and longed for had come at last and she wondered what her mamma would have said if she had been here to share it all with her.

Chapter Twenty

As they went down the path at the side of the house she introduced herself. "I'm Velana Domingo, I come from Olhão in southern Portugal . . . and . . ." Taking a deep breath she blurted out the words she had been waiting to say for a long time. "I think – oh, I don't think, I know – I'm your daughter. You – you are my father. My Papa Mario brought me up as his own and it was only when he died that I found out about you."

McKinnon stopped in his tracks and stared at Velana. His eyes, which were a deep sea blue, widened and became filled with questioning wonder. "Velana, Velana Domingo!" he cried. "I've never heard of you till now but somehow, the moment I saw you I knew you were kin! I felt it in here." He placed his hand over his heart. "But – my daughter! I never knew you existed!"

"My mother met you in Faro when she worked there in the fish market as a young girl . . ."

"Theresa," he whispered. "Your mother's name was Theresa? Am I right?"

Velana nodded and said, "Yes, and still is."

"Ah, we were so much in love, it was truly a whirlwind romance. I've often thought about her, my little mermaid, but alas it was over too soon. I sailed away from her, back here to Corrish where I married my late wife and settled down to raise our three daughters. Heather, the youngest whom you already met at the front door, Iona and Kirsty who are around somewhere. But what am I doing, standing here babbling when I've just discovered a brand new daughter and such a beauty at that."

He smiled at her with tears in his eyes and held his arms out to her and somehow she couldn't find it in herself to resent him or blame him for any of the traumas that had recently happened.

Instead, she, too, started to cry and as they held each other in a warm embrace that somehow bridged the years, Bracken ran round them in circles, whimpering and wondering at all the fuss, yet sensing that Velana was someone wonderful and part of the family circle.

It took Ian McKinnon a few minutes to gain control of himself but when he did he held Velana away and said huskily, "I know that you're my daughter but I don't want you to call me Father or Dad or anything like that; none of the girls do, they've always just called me Ian and that's the way I like it."

"Well I don't know about that," Velana teased, "I like the sound of Dad, but I suppose Ian will have to do for now." She took his hand. "Come on, I've got another surprise for you, you might as well get them all at once."

She led him towards the Range Rover and after introducing him to Guida and Collette she got them to help her lift the babies in their carrycots out of the back seat and place them on the garden bench under a window which was surrounded by beautiful, sweet-smelling, sandal roses.

Velana indicated the babies. "Your grandchildren," she said simply, "Edward and Eva. Mamma hasn't seen them yet but I hope she will before very long."

She plucked the babies out of their cots and handed them to her father. He took them both into the powerful circle of his arms and gazed down at them in wonderment, presenting a striking picture to those who watched.

He was a fine figure of a man in his forties, youthful-looking for his age, more than six feet tall and very erect, with thick fair hair swept straight back from his forehead, a broad muscular build, and eyes that were very blue when he looked at Velana and said, "This is one of the most wonderful moments in my life. Wait till the girls see their new-found nephew and niece, they're not going to believe it."

As if on cue, his three daughters appeared. On seeing Velana one of them let out a little squeal of delight. "Velana! Velana Domingo! I'd recognise you anywhere. I'm your number one fan. I've got all of your tapes and records."

Ian's eyes opened wide with surprise. "My God!" he exclaimed, "this is all getting beyond me. Not only do I discover I've got another daughter but now it appears she's a famous one at that. Trust Kirsty to recognise you. She keeps up to date with everything that's going on in the world and before I lose track of things altogether, I want you to meet the rest of the family."

He introduced the girls in turn. Iona, a beautiful brunette with dark green, hypnotic eyes and a reserved manner; Kirsty, a bubbly redhead with flashing blue eyes and a radiant smile; Heather, the youngest at sixteen, well-built, with tight, curly, fair hair and a capable air about her.

They were gazing quizzically at Velana and Ian quickly explained everything to them. For a moment they stared at her in astonishment, lost for words, then they hugged one another while Guida and Collette looked on, entranced by all that had happened in the last few minutes.

"You will stay of course, all of you," Ian said with a laugh. "We'll squeeze you in somehow, the girls won't mind doubling up. Come away in, this calls for a celebration."

Still holding the twins in his strong arms, he led the way inside. The visitors glanced round them in delight. It was like stepping back in time. The room was filled with shining timbers and chandlery salvaged from ships that had been wrecked on the island's rugged coastline. The large, open stone fireplace, had a thick, solid oak mantelpiece mounted on top, the floors were of highly-polished timber decking but the biggest feature of all was the timbered staircase and banister which had been salvaged in one piece from the saloon of some ancient ship.

"What a beautiful house," Collette said appreciatively. "It really is out of this world, alive and lived in and so nautical it's like being on board ship."

"My great grandfather built it over a hundred years ago," Ian said proudly. "It's been handed down through the family ever since." Turning to Velana he smiled and told her, "This is your home whenever you want it to be. No matter where you travel there will always be a place here for you."

He placed his hand on hers and she knew that he meant every word he said; sincerity was in his voice, she could see it in his eyes, the warmth of his smile reached out to her and a feeling of happiness pervaded her heart.

Kirsty called from upstairs. "Come up and see your rooms. I've prepared two at the front facing the sea."

The top of the house presented more surprises. A huge ship's wheel hung from the ceiling with lights all around its rim; even the bedrooms were more like ships officers' cabins than anything else, with polished wood lining the walls, little portholes in the doors, built-in wardrobes and double bunks in each room.

"Make yourself comfortable," Kirsty told Velana after she had shown Guida and Collette into the room they would be sharing. "I'll see to your baggage and the babies' carrycots." She was excited about her new-found famous sister and wanted to ask her lots and lots of questions, starting off by saying, "What's it like to sing in front of all those thousands of people? Don't you ever get nervous? I think I'd faint or my legs would turn to jelly just thinking about it."

"I do get nervous beforehand," Velana agreed, "but I'm quite used to it now and take it in my stride. I love my work and I love singing and when I'm on stage I feel in control of things. It wasn't always like that though; it was Guida who gave me confidence and taught me stagecraft and polish. She's a wonderful person and a wonderful musician; I don't know what I'd do without both her and Collette, they're always there for me, and made me see how important it is to have good, true friends in your life."

Kirsty nodded eagerly, "I hope I can be your friend as well as being your sister."

"I'm sure you will be," Velana said softly. "We've got a lot of catching up to do, I can hardly take it in yet, meeting my real father, three new sisters to get to know – we'll all need time to get used to one another."

"I feel I know you very well already," Kirsty said enthusiastically and reluctantly left the room to see how the other guests were faring.

By the time Velana had freshened up and gone back downstairs, Heather and Iona had fed and changed the babies and were sitting with them in armchairs in front of the fire.

"I hope you don't mind," was Iona's greeting as Velana came in, "it seemed the right thing to do."

"Of course I don't mind; you can feed them any time you like – after all," she giggled, "you're their aunties and it's better that they should get to know you right away." She looked at Iona. "Was it you I heard singing just now? It sounded lovely?"

Iona reddened a little. "It was me, and it's called the cradle song."

Quietly she began to sing it again; Velana picked it up, and they both started humming it together in harmony, their voices blending like the beautiful pipes of Pan.

Ian, who was outside gathering logs and peats for the fire, stopped for a moment and listened. Bending down he patted Bracken who was never far from his side. "Listen, lad, the McKinnons are singing. I think we'll have a ceilidh tonight. It's a time for celebration."

The dog looked up at his master and gave a little bark of approval then followed him to the gate where a neighbour had stopped for a chat. It was a good chance for Ian to mention the ceilidh. He knew it wouldn't be long before the island telegraph passed the word around.

Chapter Twenty-one

The McSweens weren't really helping each other. After Velana's departure for Corrish that morning Hamish had felt pangs of remorse at the way he had handled the situation, and to make amends he had attempted to try and ease the tension between him and his parents.

But it was to no avail. The minister seemed hell-bent on spreading doom and gloom till the atmosphere became so thick you could have cut it with a knife. He kept mumbling on about the demons of temptation that had driven Maud to a fatal destiny, telling her she had fallen into an abyss of depravity and sin in her seeking the doubtful comforts of another man's bed.

"After that you tried to hide in God's house!" he accused her, his voice booming out as if he was preaching to his congregation. "Pretending to the world that you were a worthy disciple of His when for years you were living a lie! Both to the Almighty and to your own son. Now this terrible thing has come upon us and only the Lord knows where it will all end."

"Leave Mother alone!" Hamish cried out in an agony of tortured mind. "Can't you see she's already suffered enough from all this? She's always been lenient with you and put you and your church work first. She listened to you and helped you but you never did the same with her. Can't you forgive and forget? We're all affected by the things that have happened, not just you. You're destroying us all with your bitterness instead of trying to help us to see a way out. I can't listen to any more of it, I'm going out for some air."

His voice was ragged and strange to his own ears. He hardly saw where he was going when he marched through the hallway, slamming the door behind him. Maud, sitting at the kitchen table, jumped with fright as the sound of her son's departure reverberated through the house. Depression settled on her like a black cloak and lowering her head she fell once more to sobbing, knowing in her heart that she wouldn't get any comfort from her husband, who was beyond all such feelings.

He was now pacing up and down, wringing his hands, reciting passages from some of his own sermons, uncaring about anything or anyone but himself as he ranted and raved and went on at his wife without mercy.

Hamish wandered past the village and down to the harbour. The tide was out and he strolled on to the shingle beach to be alone with his thoughts. The crunching of shells under his feet felt good as he paced out along the tideline around the curving bay, passing some of his old haunts where he used to play as a child in the shallow caves below the cliff-face on the headland.

Blindly he wandered on, his father's outbursts still ringing in his ears, thoughts of Velana and his children filling his mind. What would become of them all now? They had shared so much; the love he had felt for her had been fulfilling and wonderful. Now, it seemed, theirs had been an unholy union, one that should never have been – never would be again . . .

A sob escaped him. He couldn't go on without her; he would rather die than be parted from her . . . from his darling little girl . . . his son . . .

He approached an old beachcomber who was gathering timber among the flotsam and jetsam on the shore, piling it high above the tideline near one of the caves which he had commandered and improvised into his home. He was an old man with a dark, weather-beaten face that resembled a burnt walnut; although his clothes were tattered and torn there was a sparkle in his eyes, a wisdom in his expression, a gentle aura about him that gave the impression of one who knew things that other people didn't.

"The clouds are gathering," he greeted Hamish quietly, "I think we're in for a wild one." Even as he spoke it started to rain, softly at first, then more relentlessly, driven by a fierce wind that began to whip the sea into a turmoil of foamy, crashing waves.

"Come and get some shelter," the old man called out above the wind as he began making his way up to the cave.

Hamish hesitantly followed him and watched as he threw some wood on top of a glowing fire, an action which sent sparks floating up a natural chimney inside the rock face.

"I'm Sandy Burk," the old man introduced himself. "Warm yourself, son, you look tired, you don't have to speak if you don't want to."

In silence, Hamish held his hands to the fire and stared into it while the old man busied himself by swinging his cooking pot over the flames. To make conversation he began to speak about a trailing light that he had seen earlier on in the day, falling from the sky towards the houses in the village.

"It was a sign," he whispered in his deep Highland voice, "a sign that there will soon be death and tragedy in the house it touched. It is written in the legends of the islands that the trailing light which resembles the tail of a comet is a ladder leading to heaven for the soul to travel on."

Hamish swung round to face the old man, his eyes almost popping out of his head. "No," he whispered harshly, "don't speak like that, please, don't speak like that."

Sandy Burk stared at him and said softly, "You have a troubled mind, lad, tell me what ails you and I might be able to help."

But Hamish backed away from him. "No, it's too late, I can't face it, I can't . . ." Then he cried out in anquish, "Mother! Oh, Mother . . ."

Repeating her name over and over he ran out of the cave into the howling gale to make his way along the wind-lashed beach. In seconds he was soaked to the skin but the buffeting didn't seem to bother him as he drove himself on towards the manse, muttering, "Mother, Mother" over and over again.

But he didn't stop at the manse, sitting dark and forbidding on top of the knoll, instead he carried on towards the church which was in total darkness.

The heavy, arched timber door squeaked on its hinges as he pressed against it to open it. All was quiet as he entered the dark interior of the church; only the sound of the gale howling and wailing outside disturbed the grey-black silence.

The McKinnon croft was filling up with people from all over the island, who, having heard there was to be a ceilidh, came on horseback, in jeeps and trucks, on bikes and tractors – anything they could get their hands on. Ian was at the door to welcome them and introduce them to Velana who was standing by his side. Earlier on in the day she had unburdened some of her fears to him, telling him about Hamish and the terrible outcome of Maud's confession. Ian had gone pale with shock on hearing all this, telling her he had never meant to hurt anyone by his deeds of long ago, the results of which seemed to be piling in on top of him all at the same time.

"I won't make excuses for myself," he had said huskily. "I was young, I had a lot of love to give, and I shared it as young people do. But fate has a peculiar way of working and I wasn't to know what uncanny twists it had in store. It's all been so sudden. At the moment my mind's in a whirl and I can't think straight." At that point he had gathered her hands in his to add, "The birth of any baby is a blessing . . . and you, my daughter, are a classic example of that; I would never intentionally hurt you, you must believe that, and I would hate to lose you just when I have found you."

In some strange way, Velana was comforted by his words, and able in some small measure to look forward to meeting some more of the islanders that evening. Hamish was uppermost in her mind, however – she was longing to see him again so that she could comfort him and tell him how much he would always mean to her.

But in the busy whirl of preparations for the ceilidh there was little time to spare for moping, and now the house was filling up with people bearing gifts of cake, bread, whisky, some of them carrying in plates of cooked duck, chicken, and salmon. Old Tom, the postie, and his wife Jean, the postmistress, both plump and smiling, had brought their fiddles, all tuned up and ready to start playing, and it wasn't long before a lively rendition of 'Scotland the Brave' had everyone up dancing, their whirling feet making the timber flooring creak and groan beneath them.

Guida and Collette, really impressed by the traditional dances, were soon persuaded to join in. When

Tom announced 'The Dashing White Sergeant' they were seized by one of the young farmers who led them into position as the lively melody filled the room. Soon they were yelping and screaming with delight as they tried to learn the intricate steps in an atmosphere of pure laughter and happiness.

After that, Roderick McLeod, the local carpenter, very impressive in his full Highland dress, played selections on his bagpipes, marching up and down the room in time to the music.

Velana was thrilled as she listened. The hairs rose on the back of her neck, shivers ran down her spine, her Scottish blood was rising and a strong feeling of pride rushed through her veins. She had never expected it to happen; now that it had she knew that she was experiencing some of the most wonderful moments of her life, and tears were in her eyes when Roderick stopped playing to thunderous applause.

There was a lull after that, one in which it was announced that Murdo Munro was going to tell everyone a story, whereupon a small man with dark bushy eyebrows and piercing eyes, ambled over to the fireplace to tap his pipe out against the metal hob and to slowly fill it from an old tobacco tin that he fished from his pocket.

Only then did he start to speak, in a deep voice, his eyes faraway as he began. "The story I am about to tell you is true. It happened long ago in tragic circumstances when a fishing boat sank with all hands, leaving many young widows. They all had little bairns to look after, except one. Her name was Morag; she was sad and lonely and very depressed. One day she was out for a walk along the beach and she found a baby seal lying on the shore a bit distressed-looking, so she took it home and nursed it like a real human baby, placing it in a cradle by the fireside and feeding it on sheep's milk from a baby's bottle."

At this point Murdo fondled his pipe with his large hands and poked tobacco into the bowl with a stained forefinger while everyone urged him to go on with his tale. Shaking his head sorrowfully he continued in a breathy voice, "The next morning, Morag went over to the cradle expecting to see the young seal, but in its place was a real live baby girl and lying beside the cradle on the floor was an empty seal pelt. She was a beautiful child and Morag nursed her and looked after her, so happy to have been blessed with a bairn at last.

"She called the little girl Sally and as she grew up, Morag taught her to sing and speak in the Gaelic and to knit and sew and help with all the chores in the croft. They could sing beautifully together, accompanying themselves on the harp, and soon they became renowned all over the islands and the mainland. When they practised their singing on the beach near the croft, the locals would come up from the village and the seals would swim in from the sea to lie on the rocks and listen to the wonderful singing and playing by Morag and Sally.

"But one of the islanders was terribly jealous of them and in her hatred she struck Sally down with an axe one night when she was alone on the beach, killing her instantly. The perpetrator of the terrible deed crept away into the darkness, and no one knew who had committed the shocking crime."

Murdo leaned over and lifting a burning ember from the fire he lit his pipe with it and puffed away loudly which made him cough and splutter even louder. He cleared his throat and spat into the fire, making sparks fly with a sizzling sound while everyone waited patiently for him to go on with the story.

"Well, poor Morag, she was devastated and died the very next day of a broken heart," Murdo intoned, his voice hollow and quivering. "The villagers buried them together in the same grave in the garden of their little croft where they had spent so many happy years. The murderer was finally found by the villagers in her croft, lying on the floor screaming at the top of her voice that she had seen seals dancing in the middle of her living room, calling out her name. She confessed to killing Sally, before she herself finally died of the fright, her eyes bulging out of her head and her hair turning white as the driven snow overnight. All over the croft, the villagers found webbed footprints, and an empty seal pelt was lying on the bed."

Murdo lowered his voice to an eerie whisper, "To this day, as evening fades into night, the voices of Morag and Sally can sometimes be heard, singing above the sound of the surf."

As the story came to an end, old Tom raised his fiddle and played some haunting minor notes, adding to the drama of the finale. Murdo raised his bushy eyebrows and stared at the audience with his piercing eyes and smiled a smile that was almost sinister, as good-natured clapping broke out, accompanied by the stamping of feet on the wooden floor.

Chapter Twenty-two

When Murdo had finished his tale, Velana went upstairs to check on the twins, but she needn't have worried, Eva and Edward were sound asleep in their little carrycots, undisturbed by the din below. Velana kissed them both on their soft, warm cheeks before slipping back out of the room to go downstairs.

Halfway down she paused, the sound of a beautiful tenor voice, singing 'Ae fond Kiss' floated up to her. Quietly she went into the living room to see her father, standing there singing his heart out, and in that instant she realised where she had acquired her vocal talents. Pride swelled in her breast as she looked around the room and saw that there was hardly a dry eye to be seen as the words of the lovely ballad soared poignantly out from Ian McKinnon's throat.

Guida caught Velana's eye and nodded her approval at the way Ian reached the high notes with such ease and Velana wasn't surprised when everyone asked for more as soon as he had finished.

Turning, he looked at Velana. "Come and join me," he said softly. She went to stand beside him; he nodded over to old Tom who started to play 'Hear My Song'. Ian sang the melody while Velana sang in harmony. Their combined voices were like angels in a heavenly choir, so soft and beautiful yet so powerful and professional; the atmosphere in the room was electric.

Father and daughter made a striking picture, he so tall and fair, she so slender and lovely with her shining blonde hair flowing down her back. When they finished there was silence for a few moments before appreciative clapping broke out and some of the young crofters, who had been secretly admiring Velana, took the opportunity to kiss her and shake her hand.

The 'Boston Two Step' was next on the agenda, with Bridie McNab and the piermaster's wife seizing their chance to do a clog dance. As soon as the music started they were off, clippity-clopping round the room, Bridie kicking her heels up as she kept time to the music. It was while she was doing this that one of her clogs came off, sailing across the room like a rugby ball and smashing through the front window, out into the garden.

No one expected it to be returned by a tall, dark figure who suddenly filled the doorway, none other than Sergeant Gray the island policeman, holding the clog in his hand.

"What's all this then?" he said sternly, looking at Bridie standing there wearing only one clog. A ghost of a smile touched his face as he returned the errant item of footwear to its owner. There were shouts for him to join the party and have a dram, but he shook his head and explained that he was still on duty, before walking over to Ian to tell him that he was here on official business and was looking for a lady called Velana Domingo.

Ian beckoned to his daughter and introduced her to the policeman whose expression was very grave as he shook her hand. "Could we go somewhere quieter to speak?" he asked, including Ian in his enquiry.

Ian led the way out of the room to a small study across the hall and made to go out again when Sergeant Gray said it was alright if he stayed.

"It might be better in the circumstances, Sir," the

policeman said politely, then turning to Velana he went on. "I'm afraid I've got some very bad news for you, Miss Domingo. It seems that Hamish McSween, son of the minister of Layish, has been found dead there. I'm very sorry to be the bringer of this news as I believe that you and the lad were sweethearts . . ."

Velana stared at him. He was still talking, she could see his mouth moving but she couldn't hear the words; it was as if her head was inside a tunnel and a train was roaring through, as she almost blacked out . . .

"Velana." Just in time Ian caught hold of her and led her gently over to a chair where she sat white-faced as the sergeant went on in a solemn voice.

"It was his father who found him in the church; there will be further investigations of course, but according to our enquiries it looks as though the lad took his own life and hung himself from the church altar."

Something in Velana's mind seemed to snap. "How could he, how could he?" she cried out in anguish. "How could he leave us like this? Me? His children? It's not true, none of it is true. You're making it up! I know you're making it up!" Staggering to her feet she weakly pummelled the sergeant's chest with her clenched fists, sobbing as she did so, the sound growing in volume till the small room was filled with it.

"Hush, lass, hush." Ian gathered her to the great wall of his chest to stroke her hair and murmur soothing words of comfort, leaving the sergeant to go and tell the rest of the family what had happened.

Not long after that the ceilidh guests silently took their leave and before the sergeant, too, departed he told Velana, "I'll escort you back to Layish first thing in the morning. I've arranged for the police launch to pick us up at the jetty – meanwhile . . ." He placed a sympathetic hand on her arm. "You must try and rest, this has been a terrible blow to you and it's as well that you've got family round you at a time like this."

Velana bit her lip and nodded, before slowly making her way upstairs, followed closely by Guida and Collette who were devastated by the news she had just received.

"You must be feeling as if the world's collapsed," Guida said gently. "But the sergeant's right, you have to try and get some sleep, it's going to be a long day tomorrow. Don't worry about anything, we'll be close by your side and will look after you and the twins."

"I've turned down your bed." Collette came out of the room. "And Kirsty says she'll bring up some cocoa to help you relax."

Velana knew she wouldn't sleep that night, but it was so good to know that she was surrounded by a family who cared and friends like Guida and Collette who were always there when she needed them. With tears in her eyes she hugged them both before going in to gaze down at her sleeping babies and wonder what the future held in store for them.

It had been a long-drawn-out three days since Velana had received the tragic news and circumstances of Hamish's death. With the help of Ian and her sisters she had made all the funeral arrangements, since the minister and Maud were in no fit state to do anything and couldn't even attend the church service.

Both of them had been hospitalised; in the minister's case for a very long time. His mental state had deteriorated and he had suffered a complete nervous breakdown – the shock of finding Hamish's body in the church having all but pushed him over the edge. Maud, on the other hand, was disquietingly calm. She hadn't asked any questions but seemed to have retreated into a shell of her own making and it was going to take a lot of tender loving care and understanding before she would ever get mentally well again.

The minister from Corrish had been brought over to Layish to conduct the funeral service. It was a sad, solemn occasion which many of the islanders attended and the church was filled to capacity. Velana was escorted by Ian and her sisters, Guida and Collette following behind with the twins.

The minister, who was a young man, spoke highly of Hamish, saying he was one of the island's sons who had left to seek his fortune; now he had returned only to make another journey, a journey to the eternal light. "For who can condemn a man for taking his own life when it is the sickness of the mind that has taken him, just as any kind of sickness of the body. May God bless his soul and the young family that he has left behind. Amen."

The congregation echoed the minister's prayers, giving Velana their support. She still felt quite numb and had visions of Hamish, hanging from the altar, alone in the last moments of his life. The memory of seeing him lying on the cold slab in the mortuary was vivid. She had pressed her lips against his face, as if trying to awaken him from his final sleep, though she knew he was gone forever. All she had left of him now were the twins, they were part of him. They, and her new-found family on Corrish, would give her the hope and strength to carry on.

After laying Hamish to rest in the little churchyard, the funeral party headed back to Corrish. Velana had arranged with the lawyers on Layish to handle the estate; she had also made extra arrangements for Maud and the minister to be well looked after, in hospital and beyond, as they would both need long-term treatment.

Velana took one last look at Layish village before the ferry sailed round the headland, and it vanished from view. She knew that part of her heart would always be there on that island with the man who had given her so much happiness and love.

"Great news!" Collette turned excitedly to Velana as she put down the phone. "That was Mr Santos on the line. Before we start recording in the autumn he'd like you to do another European tour, starting in Ireland, then France, Germany, and most of the Scandinavian countries. It would be a tight schedule but we could do rehearsals here on the island in the next couple of weeks."

"Sounds good." Velana spoke without enthusiasm. "But I'll need to think about it, I don't feel ready for work just yet."

"It's exactly what you do need," Collette said firmly, "some work to keep your mind off things. It's been over two weeks since the funeral and you can't keep moping about forever. You'll have to try and get back to normal, for your own sake and for the sake of the twins . . . also, Guida and I can't hang around here much longer. We've had our break; it's time to go."

"Oh stop trying to boss me about!" Velana suddenly lost her temper. "I'll start work when I'm good and ready and I don't need you to tell me what to do!" Lifting her anorak off the hook in the hall she stormed out of the house with Bracken following a few paces behind her as she headed up the glen.

Her mind was in a turmoil, she felt at a loose end but couldn't face the thought of working again. She hadn't meant to be angry with Collette. Already she felt sorry for snapping at her and vowed that she would apologise to her when she got back. As she climbed the steep bank leading on to the moor it started to rain heavily, followed by a fierce wind driving the droplets of water into her face. For a moment she thought about turning back, but it was only a heavy shower; the sky soon cleared and the sunlight began flickering through the rain, shining on the moorland heather and summer grasses, gleaming on the sheer rock face of the cliffs, making them look as if they had been polished by the passing, low-lying clouds.

She made her way along the well-worn path running across the moorland where an abundance of wild flowers delighted her eye: red poppies, primroses, celandines, yellow flags, and corn marigolds, all scattered over the spreading landscape.

Thoughts of home in Olhão came to her mind: her mother, Father Silvas, Jose especially. She wondered how he was getting on in the world of the clergy. She knew deep down in her heart she still adored him and would always love him in a very special way. This place she was standing in reminded her of the poppy field where she and Jose had made love for the very first time. She felt a warm glow rising in her cheeks as she glanced at the wild red poppies dotted so profusely on the rugged landscape, like some multi-coloured magic carpet. The cool, sweet scents of the wild flowers swept up the valley, the whispering wind in her face made her feel wild and free; she sat down on top of a rock that was shaped like a stool and in meditation she reached inside herself in silent peace for what seemed like an eternity.

She gave a start as Bracken licked her hand and lifted her arm with his nose, letting her know it was time to go. "I know, boy," she sighed, "we have to be getting back. I'm ready now, I know what I'm going to do. I've come to a decision." She was talking to the dog but also talking to herself. "Let's go down and tell the family."

As she made her way homewards, the evening sunset glowed a rich gold behind the dark triple peaks of Corrish, reflecting on the unruffled, lustrous, velvet calm of the sea and casting purple shadows on the nearby islands. The beauty of it entranced her and she felt she couldn't get enough of it as she went down the valley and along the cliff top where seagulls, terns, and guillemots, screeched and screamed with delight as they bobbed and weaved and dived into the sea, competing for their evening meal.

Chapter Twenty-three

The McKinnon sisters were taking in the washing from the line in the back garden when Velana appeared with Bracken at her heels. "I've been for a walk on the moor and I've made a decision," was her breathless greeting. "How would you all like to go to Portugal for a holiday?"

The girls looked at one another in wonderment, for once lost for words. Kirsty was the first to speak. "How soon can we go?" she enquired excitedly.

"We'll fly out as soon as everything can be arranged. I'd love you to meet my mother and I know you'll love Olhão."

"You really mean it?" gasped Iona.

"Of course I mean it," Velana laughed.

"We'll have to get some new clothes." Kirsty began making rapid plans. "And find someone to look after the croft and the animals and the chickens . . ."

Velana went indoors, leaving her sisters prancing and dancing around the garden with delight, shouting, "Yippee!" and "Yahoo!"

Collette was in the hall as Velana entered. "Collette," she acknowledged, looking rather shamefaced. "I'd like to apologise for snapping at you earlier. I knew you were right, I do need to get back to work and that's exactly what we're going to do – but first we're all going to Portugal to visit my mother. I'm longing to see her and for her to see the twins."

Collette put her arms around Velana. "I understand," she said warmly, "and I'm sorry for sounding bossy, I was just trying to help. I'd do anything for you, you know that, don't you?"

"Yes, I know that," Velana said huskily. "You and Guida have been wonderful and I couldn't ask for better friends. I'd trust you with my life."

"I'll go and make the arrangements at once," Collette decided just as Ian came in from the garden carrying the twins.

A beaming smile was on his face as he said, "So we're all going to Portugal? It sound wonderful, if a little sudden, but I'm sure we can work something out." Gazing down at Eva and Edward he added softly, "And you, my sweethearts, are going to see your grandmamma at last. How does that suit you?"

Bracken started to yelp and wag his tail, wanting to be part of whatever was going on and he seemed to understand when Ian patted his head and told him regretfully that he had to stay behind and look after the house while everyone was away.

"Who will you get to look after the place?" asked Velana.

"My cousin, Alex McPhee, and his wife. They've done it before and know where everything is better than I do myself. They love coming here and the animals will be well looked after."

Guida was sitting in a corner of the room with her keyboard, engrossed in running through a composition she had been working on. As her deft fingers floated across the keys a wonderful sound came tinkling out and Velana could tell that the older woman had been influenced by the beauty and magic of the Hebridean islands. She had the gift for drawing on beautiful things and injecting them into her music with a feeling that was totally moving. Iona came into the room and stood for a moment, listening to Guida's wonderful playing, then she took her flute out of its case and assembled it. Raising it to her lips she blew gently at first, following the melody with ease, then she played some deep natural harmonies, her green eyes sparkling as if they were dancing to the music, her fingers moving like lightning, her body swaying to and fro, her whole being absorbed in the rhythym of the music.

Both Guida and Velana sensed the natural power of her playing and when the score was finished Guida said enthusiastically, "That was wonderful, why don't you come and join the band? You are certainly good enough, and I'm sure Velana would be delighted if you did."

Velana agreed with her. "Anyone who can play like that can accompany me any time, and not just because you're my sister. We would make a great team together."

Iona was delighted and rushed out to the garden to tell the others about her chance to go on the road with Velana. "Oh, I wish I could come too," Kirsty said a little enviously.

"We can't all be great musicians," said Heather wisely. "Iona has been playing the flute since she was a little girl and she has always been good at it, now this is her big chance."

Iona placed the flute to her lips again and, like the Pied Piper, she began to play and dance at the same time while Kirsty and Heather began prancing round the drying washing, Bracken joining in the fun, barking and running after their legs till he got entangled with them and they all fell over like a row of skittles to land in a laughing heap on top of one another, Bracken seizing his chance to give their faces a good licking.

* * *

Collette had soon made the travel arrangements. "That's it, we're all set," she said as she put the phone down. "The helicopter will be here the day after tomorrow which should give us enough time to get packed. We'll be leaving early morning and could have a few hours in Glasgow before the flight to Portugal. We could maybe do some shopping, I've heard there are some lovely big department stores in the centre of the city.

Velana felt a surge of excitement welling up within her – she loved shopping – but the fact that she was going home to visit her mother really gladdened her heart. Collette read her mind. "I've contacted your mother, she knows we are coming. I've also arranged for two mobile homes to be delivered to the farm so we will all have a place to sleep."

"That's a great idea," said Velana, "you always think of the right things to do."

"That's my job, to try and make things run as smoothly as possible. We'd better start packing, there's lots to do and plenty of last minute chores to see to." As she was speaking she had picked up her portfolio and one or two of her paintings fluttered to the floor. Velana, bending to pick them up, was captivated by the vibrant beauty of the watercolour scenes. One in particular held her attention; it was a landscape, painted high up on the moor, silvered with moonlight that shone through breaks in the low-lying cloud, the rays lighting distant gullies below the triple peaks, leaving others in purple shadow lower down the glen. In the foreground, a magnificent stag was standing on a rock, apprehensive-looking, poised ready for action against the young bucks who were hovering in the background, his little herd of hinds feeding nearby.

"This is perfect," Velana said as she studied the painting, "so simple yet so powerful. You've captured the true meaning of nature with a few strokes of your brush, its so vibrant and alive . . ."

She paused. Somehow the picture reminded her of Hamish when he was happy and carefree, before tragedy struck and his mind had snapped . . . In those moments she could feel his loneliness, the desperation that had made him do what he did . . . "Oh God!" she cried, biting her lip to stem her tears. "Here I am, making plans to go home – while my darling Hamish lies in the cold soil of his island. I feel, sometimes, that I could die too – he so loved life . . ."

Collette's ever-comforting arms were ready. "Come on now," she whispered, "you'll have to stop dwelling on the dark side of life. Hamish is out of reach of uncertainty and care, you must look forward, you've got so much to live for and your babies need you." She smiled a warm smile and added, "Speak of the sun and its rays appear, the painter proposes and the mind disposes . . . and with these few words of wisdom . . ." Lifting the rest of the scattered paintings she bundled them neatly together and placed them in their folders and said briskly, "Now, let's get on with the packing or we'll never be ready in time."

Chapter Twenty-four

The surge of the engine noise drowned out all other sounds as everyone climbed into the helicopter and strapped themselves in, assisted by the co-pilot. Ian waved out of the window to his cousin Alex McPhee who would be looking after the place while they were gone. Bracken had not come to see his master off, he was hiding underneath the wood pile at the side of the house and there he stayed, petrified by the noisy metal monster that had invaded his domain.

The helicopter lifted, Velana held her children close as they flew into the misty morning sky above Corrish. She took one last look at the island before it disappeared from view under a blanket of cloud. As they gained altitude, she could see the three fingers of the triple peaks, poking up through cloud, as if beckoning her to return. She knew she would; some day she knew she would return to those golden Hebridean islands that had captured her heart for all time.

But for now, new adventures lay ahead. As they approached Glasgow under a clear summer sky, Kirsty called out, "Look at those tall buildings, they're enormous compared with our houses in Corrish."

The co-pilot nodded. "Yes, and we're going to land on top of the tallest, the Wilton Hotel's got a helipad and we'll be touching down in a couple of minutes."

The white circle of the landing pad came into view.

Kirsty gulped. "It looks like a large dartboard, I hope we can land in the middle, it seems so small from here."

The co-pilot put her at her ease, telling her they'd done it countless times and conditions were good that day. A short while later they landed dead centre of the helipad with hardly a bump to let them know that the feat had been accomplished. The hotel manager and porter were waiting to escort them to the lift; within minutes they were at street level and the manager pointed out all the best stores for them to visit.

"Right, everybody," Velana said, "let's go shopping, but remember we all have to stick together – if anyone gets lost in a store, stand at the entrance and wait, or make your way back to the hotel."

The excitement of shopping was like a fever; they were all caught up in it as they went round the department stores for clothes, shoes, jewellery, baby clothes, and all the accoutrements, trying everything on and having a whale of a time.

Kirsty fell in love with motifed jeans and Velana told her to get as many pairs as she liked since everything would be charged to her account and they could all have a mad spree and enjoy themselves.

Ian said he was going down to the men's department to try on some shoes and told them to stay where they were till he got back.

"Don't worry, we'll be a while yet," laughed Heather as she held up another dress and admired herself in the mirror. "I'll have to try this one on," she added and made a beeline for the changing room.

Kirsty and Iona between them were looking after the twins, the others were browsing at different counters quite a distance away. It was while Kirsty was looking at a jacket that one of the assistants, a tall, short-haired blonde wearing dark glasses, came over and said, "I'll hold the baby if you like and let you try that on."

"Oh, thanks," Kirsty said gratefully, "I won't be a minute." She handed Eva to the assistant and slipped on the jacket. "How does it look from the back?" she asked, but there was no answer. Turning round she saw with horror that the woman had vanished with the baby and in a panic she began looking along the clothes racks, but it was in vain, and she called out to Velana that someone had taken the baby.

The other assistants came over with the manageress who asked Kirsty what the woman had looked like and when Kirsty told her she shook her head and said there was no one with that description working there. She then went to her office and pressed the emergency switch on her desk and the alarm bells started to ring through the department store at all levels.

Ian was trying on shoes on the ground floor when the bells started ringing and, thinking it must be a fire, he made his way along towards the lift and was just about to enter it when the door of the other lift opened and out came a tall woman with short blonde hair. He stopped in his tracks, amazed to see that she was carrying baby Eva, and as she rushed past him he went after her, catching up with her as she reached the door. "Give me that baby." he said simply, "she isn't yours."

The woman turned on him in a frenzy of outrage and she began punching and kicking him. Ian's hand came up to protect himself; it caught in the woman's hair which came away in his fingers, and Ian saw that he was dealing with not a woman, but a man dressed up as one. Without ado, Ian lashed out with a powerful left hook which caught the man neatly on the chin. His legs gave way and he staggered backwards, but before he fell Ian grabbed the baby who, none the worse for her experience, was gurgling away happily and looking up at her rescuer with big, blue, wondering eyes.

A crowd had formed, encircling the man who was just coming round. The security guards arrived and after Ian told them what had happened, two of them lifted the would-be kidnapper to his feet, handcuffed him, and led him away.

"Well done, Sir," one of the guards nodded. "You'd better make your way up to the fourth floor, your family are waiting for you. I've notified them that we've caught the culprit and the baby is all right."

As the lift door opened at the fourth floor, a blur of relieved faces welcomed him. Velana was the first to throw her arms around him and the baby, while Kirsty cried in the background and declared that it had all been her fault for handing the baby over to a stranger.

"It's nobody's fault," Velana said generously. "I'm just glad that we've got Eva back and no harm has come to her. Let's finish off our shopping and get back to the hotel for lunch."

But by then, the news had spread throughout the store and everybody knew who Velana was. The assistant in the music department had her music tapes on display and now she played them on the loudspeaker system so that her voice echoed everywhere singing the haunting melody, 'Que Deus Me Perdoe'.

Kirsty looked proudly at Velana and thought, This is my sister, singing to all these people; and it dawned on her just how famous Velana really was. It made Kirsty feel good inside, a feeling that was further strengthened when they got back to the hotel, laden down with parcels, to be welcomed once more by the manager who personally supervised the safe stowage of their belongings before leading them through to the dining room where they were all treated like VIPs, with waiters and waitresses buzzing round them, pouring drinks, serving food.

Halfway through the meal, Velana proposed a toast to the twins, saying that she hoped they always would be together and thanking Ian for being there at the right time to "catch the crook and save baby Eva".

"It's a lesson to us all to be more vigilant than ever," Ian responded. "After today we must never let the twins out of our sight, whatever country we happen to be in; speaking of which, I think we should make our way up to the helipad if we're to get to the airport in time, so eat up everybody – Portugal here we come!"

The noise of the helicopter engines was deafening after the quietness of the dining room, but in minutes the porters had loaded the baggage and the visitors were off, feeling that they were leaving their stomachs on top of that building, but the pilot soon levelled out and the machine flew smoothly across the city towards the airport. After they had checked in, they made their way across the tarmac where a private jet awaited them, Ian carrying a baby in each arm. The afternoon sun shone on his silvery-blond hair and flickered on his face, casting faint shadows which accentuated his strong, handsome features and defined the little laughter lines at the corners of his deep blue eyes.

Velana was fascinated at the picture he presented. This was her father, this tall, powerfully-built man who looked like a Viking warrior. She wanted to know all about him; he hadn't really talked very much about himself, but then, she reasoned, so much had happened recently – discovering who she was, seeing his grandchildren for the first time, the shock of finding out about Hamish and the tragic aftermath.

She searched his features and suddenly felt good

about herself; she was part of him, everything that she had achieved had come partially from him. She knew that his easy-going manner was a cover up for something more profound, a masculine strength, a depth of character, an air of pride that shone from his eyes and made people look at him twice. She noticed the air hostesses admiring him as he entered the plane and she began to understand how Maud and her mother had been so attracted to him.

The pilot's voice came over the intercom, welcoming them aboard and giving them the rundown on the weather report, flight time, et cetera. As they took off into the clouds above the River Clyde, Ian pointed out Dumbarton Rock and Loch Lomond below, and beyond them, the rugged mountains of Argyll.

"It's a wonderful place, this Scotland of ours," he told Velana, gently squeezing her hand. "I bet you could write some great songs about it."

"As a matter of fact, I already have. Guida has arranged one or two for our next tour. We'll be doing some rehearsals in Portugal so you can hear them there."

One of the air hostesses, coming round with drinks, asked Velana to sign the cover of one of her tapes, and after she had done that she closed her eyes and fell into a deep sleep, dreaming that she was walking along a country lane pushing the twins in a pram, a man dressed in black following her. When she quickened her pace he started to chase her and she was horrified when she saw a high cliff at the end of the lane. When she turned it was to see that the man was almost on top of her but she kept on running and leapt over the edge of the cliff with the twins in their pram. They were falling hundreds of feet into space, she could see the shoreline coming up to meet them, the jagged rocks getting nearer . . .

As they were about to be dashed onto the wet rocks below she screamed a silent scream and woke up with a start, wet with perspiration, her father holding her arm and asking anxiously if she was all right. "Just a bad dream," she said shakily. "I must have been thinking about the man in the store. How long have I been sleeping?"

"Almost four hours. We'll be landing soon, the pilot has just announced we'll be touching down in a few minutes."

Velana could hardly believe that she had slept so long but everyone else had done much the same and the twins were just beginning to stir as the plane touched down at Faro airport.

Chapter Twenty-five

Within forty minutes they were driving up the country road towards the Domingo farm. Velana could see the two large caravans parked at the side of the outbuildings, making the place look like a large ranch house. Excitement welled up inside her as she caught sight of her mother standing beside Maria at the door, together with Farmer Rodrigas, Miguel, Pedro, and Father Silvas.

As the minibus drew to a halt beside them, Velana's eyes were misty as she ran to her mother with open arms. They held on to each other, crying and laughing at the same time.

"I'm so happy to see you, my sweetheart," Theresa said with a watery sniff, "you'll never know how much I've missed you."

Velana sniffed also and wiped her eyes. "I'm home now, Mamma, and we're going to have a lovely time. But first, come and see your grandchildren."

The babies were placed in Theresa's arms. She looked down at the little faces. "Look at them, just look at how beautiful they are!" she cried, blessing both them and herself. Turning a radiant smile on Maria she shook her head and whispered, "See my wonderful grandchildren, aren't they so precious? I love them already and I've only just met them."

She and Maria enthused over the babies and might

have continued for hours had not Father Silvas intervened with his contribution of approval before saying to Velana, "My child, God bless you and your children. Welcome home. We've all been helping to get the caravans set up and into position. Mind you, I didn't do very much, I just directed operations from my battery car. Half the time, I think I was in the way, but the Rodrigas boys worked well. They have been looking after things on the farm while you've been away."

Ian took Theresa's hands, raised them to his lips, and kissed them. "Hello, Theresa," he said softly. "It's been a long time. How are you, my dear?"

Theresa looked at him, her lips forming polite words of greeting, her memory flashing back to the days when this tall, handsome stranger had come into her life. Since then her appearance had changed; she was a bit heavier, a bit greyer, but he hadn't changed so much, he was still a fine-looking man. Her breath caught in her throat . . . they were both grandparents now. Time had changed so much . . .

"Come and meet my daughters." He was speaking again, taking her hand and leading her over to Iona, Kirsty, and Heather.

Theresa took them to her bosom, a gesture that was spontaneous and loving. The girls could feel the warmth coming from her and felt at ease with her straightaway. She introduced them to Father Silvas, Maria, Farmer Rodrigas, Miguel and Pedro. Kirsty and Heather were quite taken with the two boys, so young and handsome with their tanned skin and flashing smiles. Their manner was courteous and polite, and when Pedro offered to show them round the farm the two girls jumped at the chance.

Miguel, shyer than his younger brother, didn't have much to say at first but that didn't deter Heather. "I'd love to see the lemon and orange trees," she told him, to which Miguel smiled, stroked his dark moustache, and said in his deep voice, "No problem, follow me."

The four of them went off towards the foothills bordering the farm, Maria calling after her sons to be sure and look after the girls.

"Don't worry, Mamma," Pedro threw over his shoulder, "they'll be fine with us."

The wonderful smell of home cooking was coming from the kitchen. "Come in out of the hot sun," Theresa invited the visitors. "We've got a lot to talk about. Maria and myself are preparing Cata-Plana for everyone; it's a traditional Portuguese dish so I hope you like it."

"Smells delicious." Guida sniffed the air appreciatively as they all went inside, leaving Ian and Farmer Rodrigas to unload the luggage and amiably discuss politics and football. Ian was a good listener, showing his interest in what the other man was saying, getting his own point over from time to time. Velana was glad that they were getting on so well. They were about the same age, though Miguel senior looked older with his heavy build and a paunch that wobbled up and down when he laughed his jolly laugh.

Velana had brought gifts for everyone and after dinner, when she had unpacked her case, she gave Father Silvas a box of six different kinds of pipes and tobacco while Miguel senior received a fine gold watch on a chain.

Maria was flabbergasted when Velana presented her with a beautiful tartan dress and matching shawl. "I hope it fits," Velana said a little doubtfully, eyeing the older woman's generous proportions.

"Oh Velana," Maria gasped, "I'll make sure it fits, even if I have to starve for a month. You're so kind, I love it." She held the dress in front of her and started to dance around the room, the menfolk laughing and clapping at her antics.

"And this is for you, Mamma." Velana handed Theresa a large box. "I know you never buy yourself anything and like making your own things, but I decided it was time you had a treat."

Theresa opened the box and gasped, for it was a complete wardrobe of day clothes and evening wear, including jewellery. A little note inside read 'To a very special lady. Love, Velana.' Tears of joy shone in Theresa's eyes; she hugged her daughter and retreated to a corner of the room to stare at her new things and touch them with reverent fingers.

Collette, who had been unpacking in one of the caravans with Iona's help, came in to say, "These vans could become permanent fixtures, they're more like mobile homes with all the mod cons. I love the big living rooms – the upholstery's really plush. There's no reason why we can't set one up as a music room for our rehearsals. I've already put all the instruments in there."

"Everything is wonderful tonight," Maria beamed, throwing her tartan shawl round her shoulders and giving it a loving pat. "We should have a little celebration."

Theresa nodded her agreement and asked Miguel and Pedro if they would fetch one of the small barrels of medronho that were stored in the cellar. They soon returned, carrying between them a small wooden cask which they placed on the dresser. Theresa, crystal glasses at the ready, turned the little brass tap and out poured the golden-coloured liquid to be handed round the assembly.

"Do you remember, Velana," Theresa said quietly, "how you helped to distil this batch over three years ago with your father?"

"How could I forget, Mamma? He taught me well, especially how to control the heat of the fires at special times during the process of distillation."

Farmer Rodrigas emptied his glass, wiped his moustache, and gave a deep sigh. "That's the best medronho I've ever tasted. Mario knew how to make it, all right."

Ian was a bit more cautious, taking only a small sip to begin with, running it round his tongue before swallowing. Only then did he pass an opinion. "Tastes a bit like a good malt whisky – and that, from a Scotsman, is as good a comparison as you'll get any day."

"And you'll never suffer from a hangover after drinking medronho," laughed Farmer Rodrigas. "If you're tired, it will revive you, if you're nervous or tense it will relax you. It gives you what you need at whatever time you need it. Only the best fruit from the arbutus tree goes into it but it takes a real expert to make the brew you have just tasted. Velana knows the secrets of good medronho making, Mario saw to that."

"Amen," said Father Silvas as he finished off another glass of the golden-yellow liquid. "Pure nectar," he sighed. "God bless Mario and God bless you, Velana. You were brought up to appreciate nature's gifts and were blessed with a wonderful singing voice as well."

"I had a good teacher. Papa Mario taught me so much of what he knew, all the secrets are up here." She tapped her temple. "One day I too will pass them on, to those I trust, to my children once they are old enough to understand. If you like, I could show you, Father Silvas."

"No, no." The old man shook his silvery head. "I'll leave that to the experts. I just like to drink the stuff. It is truly one of God's gifts, to gently imbibe in moderation and be happy. I like to have a drop in black coffee at breakfast; it sets me up for the day and it eases the pain of the arthritis. The medronho that is made in bulk and sold in the supermarkets isn't as good as the home-made brew."

"The arbutus fruit is ripe and almost ready for harvesting now," Pedro put in. "If they would like to, the girls could help us pick the berries and store them in the vats for fermentation."

"Oh, I love berry-picking," Kirsty said quickly, "and I, for one, would be delighted to help with the harvest."

"That's settled then." Pedro took Kirsty's hand to squeeze it tightly while he looked lovingly into her eyes. Velana knew that look, she had seen it in Jose's eyes, when he used to look at her so adoringly. It seemed so long ago since they had romped together over the poppy field, so young and so happy. She wondered how he was getting on and she whispered to Maria if she'd had any news of him.

"I got a letter from him the other day," Maria said gently. "He is deep into his studies but he sends his love to everyone and hopes to visit some time soon."

Velana's heart missed a beat at the very thought of seeing Jose again. Deep in her heart she was still carrying a torch for him and she knew she would keep it there always . . .

The sound of Iona's flute was filling the air, spreading a feeling of pure contentment through the room. The plaintive melody of 'The Skye Boat Song' found an echo on everyone's lips, Ian taking the lead in his wonderful tenor voice, Velana accompanying, their combined voices touching everyone's hearts. Farmer Rodrigas drew his fingers through his moustache and nodded his head in appreciation of the wonderful sounds he was hearing. Theresa's eyes filled up as she listened to Ian and Velana singing together. It was as if things had turned full circle and fate had brought them all together at last.

Chapter Twenty-six

The next two weeks were hectic for Velana, Guida, and Iona, as they rehearsed for concerts and recording. Guida had been working on some new tunes and arrangements; she was a perfectionist and practised for hours on end till she was satisfied that everything was to her liking. Slowly Iona's own technique and playing power improved till it blended in beautifully with Velana's voice, Guida on the keyboard signalling that she was pleased with the sounds they were producing, Collette giving the thumbs up sign to signify her pleasure too.

"That was great," she enthused at the end of one session. "The flute makes all the difference – original and haunting and all owing itself to your magical fingers Iona. I think we've got a winner here. It's a completely different sound that we've never had before."

Iona's eyes lit up. "It really felt good and the timing was perfect. I'm no expert but I think we're as ready as we'll ever be for the real thing when it comes."

"Glad to hear it," Collette smiled at the younger girl's enthusiasm. "Mr Santos has just been on the phone and we've to leave for Dublin tomorrow. Everything's arranged for the start of the tour and it's all set up for the recording sessions. We've got a busy schedule ahead so we'd better start packing."

Velana felt excited at the thought of getting back to

work but she dreaded having to leave her mother again; the last tour had been too long and she didn't want to repeat the experience.

"Don't worry about me," Theresa tried to reassure her. "You've got to get back to work, your career is important just now. Leave the twins with me – you know I'll look after them well and they'll be quite safe here on the farm."

"Oh, Mamma," cried Velana, "that would be wonderful. I'd feel more content if they were here with you."

"That's settled then," said Theresa, smiling. "I'm delighted at the thought of having them, they'll be great company for me."

Velana spoke to Ian and told him they would be leaving in the morning, adding that he could stay on at the farm as long as he wanted.

He gave a rueful little grin. "I know Kirsty and Heather want to stay but I'll have to get back to Corrish; I've got some business to attend to, but it will just be for a little while and then I'll be back. I think Kirsty and Heather have both found love with the Rodrigas brothers. I can see it in their eyes and I'm happy for them. They're young and full of life and know what they're doing. They want to live and work on the farm and stay in Portugal for a while. They'll be a great help to Theresa and the twins."

The plane touched down at Shannon airport to a welcoming crowd of fans shouting, "Velana, we love you."

It was the first time she'd been in Ireland but her popularity through radio and television had brought her into everyone's homes and hearts. The Irish people had always been music lovers and there was a mass of happy fans waiting to catch a glimpse of Velana coming off the plane. They started to sing her hit tune, 'Que Deus me Perdoe', their voices all blending together as one. Velana waved to them as she came down the steps, laughingly pretending to conduct the singing, waving her umbrella at them, touched to see that even a sudden shower of light rain didn't dampen their spirits as they sang the heartfelt melody.

Iona felt proud to be near her famous sister among this amazing crowd and was elated to feel that she was now part of all the razzmatazz and limelight, especially when the she saw the security guards waiting to lead them through the airport terminal and into a waiting limousine, which whisked them off into Dublin city and the concert hall for a brief rehearsal for the evening's show, which was sold out.

Ten thousand fans of all ages, even mothers with children, came to hear Velana and they wouldn't let her go until she sang some Irish songs. She gladly obliged by singing 'When Irish Eyes are Smiling', and the evergreen 'Danny Boy', with Iona playing the solo part. When Velana announced that the flautist was her sister making her debut performance, the audience loved it and stamped their feet as Iona was led forward to take a bow. Iona felt as though she was floating across the stage, with Velana – her shining star – guiding her and giving her confidence. She knew she could achieve anything as long as she was close to Velana, whose glowing aura embraced everyone who came near her.

The audience and the orchestra felt it as well and gave a standing ovation, while Guida and Collette stood with their arms raised and waving, loving every minute of being on the musical road once more.

Paris, Vienna, Rome, Amsterdam. All the major cities in

Europe and Scandinavia were included on the tour with recording sessions in between and contracts clinched with film companies. It was a tight, busy schedule but they all thrived on it and were constantly on the move, from one hotel to the next – never a dull moment and not much time in which to relax.

It was on one of those rare occasions, when Iona was in the hotel room practising her scales on her flute, her fingers running up and down like two magical butterflies, that Collette came in and stood quietly listening to the haunting sound, the music overwhelming her and filling her with a delicate sense of longing and wanting.

Iona stopped playing; turning towards Collette she said in a startled voice, "Oh I thought I was alone. I was just loosening up."

For a moment their eyes met and held, then Collette came forward to take Iona in her arms and kiss her gently on the mouth, startling herself by her action and drawing back. "I'm sorry, I shouldn't have done that." She moved back a pace or two but Iona's hand on her arm stayed her.

"No, don't be sorry," the younger girl whispered with tears in her eyes. "I – I feel what you feel and have done for a long time."

"I thought you did, but I had no right to – to kiss you like that."

"You have every right." Iona pulled Collette closer, her chest rose and fell unevenly, an excitement mounting in her at the feel of Collette's warm body against her own.

"Collette, my dearest Collette," she whispered, wanting more than anything to feel again the touch of the other's lips on hers.

"Iona, my love," Collette murmured, brushing her

mouth against that of the younger girl. Warmth spread through them both like a burning flame, Iona gave a little groan as they kissed over and over till the fires within them went out of control.

Collette's lips continued their tantalising exploration of Iona's young body, lightly touching the sensitive tips of her breasts through her dress, her thumb flicking over her nipple where it strained against the silky material. In those instants of truth, Iona knew that she belonged to Collette completely. This was their moment – their admiration for one another had blossomed into a sensuous feeling of love that had been creeping upon both of them ever since they had met.

Iona wanted to speak, to pour out the love that was swelling explosively inside her, but her pounding heart gave her no breath for words; instead she submitted to the tide of sensual need cascading through her in waves of pure pleasure.

They were both naked now, shivering with a strange joy, like two delicate flowers blowing in the wind, walking hand in hand into the bedroom where their hungry desires overwhelmed them in sensations of true love and physical desires. Like two shooting stars they spiralled upwards together, fulfilling each other beyond all thought or reason, finally falling back into a plane of deep and wondrous contentment.

They lay for a long time, whispering loving endearments, their bodies wrapped together in the embrace of lovers as they sought to draw ever closer to one another.

They didn't think then of the world outside their love, a world where society in general might frown upon it, but it was a love that, for them, would never die – two adult minds and bodies, sharing and caring in a way that was precious and wonderful.

For the moment it was their secret – no one else need know about it – and although both Collette's and Iona's hearts were open and unafraid, they didn't want to do anything that would hurt Velana or her career and so they made a vow to be as discreet as possible about their feelings for one another while in the public eye.

But Velana had already guessed of their secret love. For months now she had noticed little things, they way they looked at one another, the way they talked and laughed together so warmly and intimately, and as they all sat down to dinner that evening Velana noticed the glow in them and knew in her heart that their love had been fulfilled and she was happy for them.

Later that evening, as they played to a packed audience, Iona's music was better than it had ever been, with a certain light-hearted quality about it that extended itself to the orchestra and everyone else around her.

Guida was delighted with the performance. "Everything went well tonight," she said. "I think that's the best we've played to a live audience so far on the tour. Let's keep it up, we've got three more major cities to play before our next recording session and some more film work in Milan."

Iona and Collette looked at one another. They didn't mind where they went as long as they had each other and Velana sighed a little to herself as she remembered Hamish and how good it had been when they had toured the different countries together, so much in love, so much to live for. All gone now – work was all that was left to keep her mind off what might have been. If only things had worked out differently.

Chapter Twenty-seven

The weeks ran into months and the months ran into years, with just some brief visits home to Olhão, and periodically to Corrish.

Ian was still undecided about moving to Olhão permanently, but spent a lot of his time there to be near the twins. Kirsty and Heather were now married to the Rodrigas brothers, Miguel and Pedro, and had settled down to family life on their farms. Theresa idolised Edward and Eva and was at their beck and call every minute of the day. She loved them dearly and thrived on having them near her.

She and Ian had never really got back together romantically, but they were still very close and shared in the caring of the twins, and both of them always looking forward to Velana's visits to her old home.

For the occasion of Eva and Edward's fifth birthday, Velana and the others were there to attend the weekend celebrations. Theresa had organised a party for the twins and all their playschool friends from the town, also a bus trip to the nearby Boulder Dam Lake for a picnic and games.

The twins were very popular with the locals. They were a pair of chatterboxes, always together, hand in hand, readily noticeable with their curly blonde hair, big blue eyes, and chubby red cheeks. Good-natured and smiling, they were never happier than when they were helping about the farm, and now this was their big day, made all the better because their mother and aunts were there to share it with them.

Velana was delighted to see them. She was beginning to miss them more and more when she was away on tour and wished she could be with them more often. There wasn't much room for family life in the world of show business and Velana greatly regretted that fact. She was really a country girl at heart and always would be. She loved her family dearly and knew within herself that, in the past few years, she had poured herself into her career. But now that the twins were starting to grow and would be going to school soon, she had begun to wonder if there was any other sort of career she could follow that would allow her to be near her children.

But for now, this was the twins' big day; the weather was fine if a bit overcast for the time of year. No one paid any heed to that, however; they were all out to enjoy themselves and after the candles had been blown out and the cake had been cut they were all ready for their trip up to Boulder Dam.

Ian, Pedro, and Miguel had organised the bus, and once everybody was aboard they set off up the dusty road with the children singing at the tops of their voices. The dam was about a mile above the town and as well as being a great tourist attraction during the summer months it was also the main water supply for the area.

Once there, the happy banter and chatter of the children rang in the air as they played their games, the adults taking part, running with them in the sack race, the onlookers urging them on and shrieking with laughter when Maria and Theresa tripped and rolled about helplessly on the ground.

All was happiness and relaxation; the countryside

that day was serene and peaceful. Ian looked out towards the lake that had been formed by the building of the dam. It was a vast expanse of water that spread for miles back up the valley to the mountains in the distance.

Even as Ian looked, the scene changed; suddenly the water seemed to turn grey and dark, the overcast sky became even darker, and the light breeze that had been blowing only a moment ago began to blow harder.

"Looks like there's a storm brewing," Ian called, raising his voice above the wind. "We'd better get everyone aboard the bus. I don't think it's going to let up."

"OK, children," Theresa and Maria spoke together. "Let's all get on the bus, we'll go back to the farm and finish the party there."

The rest of the womanfolk began to round up the children but Velana paused and pointed her finger towards the sea about six miles distant. She saw what looked like a tidal wave, sweeping in towards the coast and Faro on the horizon.

Ian raised his head and sniffed the wind. After years at sea he had learned how much violence and turmoil to expect in the weather, just by scenting the air, and now he felt very uneasy indeed.

The wind had started to blow in two different directions at once which was always a bad sign, sometimes bringing the most devastating storms that could last for hours. Almond and fruit trees growing close by were being tossed about, this way and that, looking as if they were going to be uprooted at any minute, while pieces of loose debris, broken roof tiles, and tree branches, began flying about overhead.

All at once, the ground began to tremble and shudder underfoot. Ian shouted over to Pedro and Miguel to forget about getting the children into the bus. "We'll have to get to higher ground and find some shelter if we can," he instructed, gazing anxiously over his shoulder to the sea in the distance.

"There's some old mine workings just above us," called Pedro, "you can see the entrance to one of them from here."

"All right. Let's get everyone up there as quickly as we can."

The earth had stopped trembling, but it was just a temporary respite. Moments later it started moving again only this time with more violence and louder rumbling than before.

"Earthquake!" Ian yelled. "Everybody up to higher ground quickly!"

He escorted some of the children up the steep bank and left them at the entrance to the mine, urgently telling them to wait there, before making his way back down the steep slope to help with the others who were crawling on their hands and knees, trying to keep their balance as best they could on ground that was quivering and starting to open up into deep fissures all around them.

"Look at the bus!" cried Kirsty. "It's tilting over."

"It's the dam!" shouted Miguel, "it's bursting!"

As he spoke, thousands of tons of concrete and giant boulders that had formed the dam, began to collapse as if it had been built with cardboard. Within seconds the bus, the road, the dam, had completely vanished under the massive weight of water that had once been the lake, and was now a raging torrent.

The ground was still shaking violently; the children were screaming as the party made their way up the steep bank, helping each other to try and keep their balance. As they reached the opening to the mine, the terrible thunderous rumbling suddenly ceased, and now all was still, except for the fierce wind and the rushing waters below, a force that was heading towards the town and engulfing everything in its path.

Ian, Pedro, and Miguel were making every effort to try and get everyone to safety away from the rushing waters and the screaming hurricane outside. Even the stale air inside the mine shaft was being stirred up; dust was flying about in clouds, making the children cough and splutter.

Theresa and Maria found an old tarpaulin lying inside the mine and they covered the children with it, improvising it into a makeshift tent into which they crawled to huddle beside the frightened youngsters. The younger women were helping the men get the rest of the children up the slope; they had formed a human chain to reach the ones farther down. Velana was desperately trying to reach a small group who had become isolated on top of the trunk of a fallen tree that was jammed against some rocks and had become an island. The turbulent waters were rushing on either side. She was trying to shout some orders to them to keep still until they could reach them. The twins were among the little group who sat huddled together, too terrified to move. The savage storm around them was the most frightening – the shrieking, howling wind overrode everything else as it kept up its unabated clamour and high-pitched intensity.

Ian realised the danger the children were in as the little island could be washed away at any moment, and he knew they would have to act fast. He plunged into the foaming waters, followed by Miguel. With a few strokes they reached the children and carried them, one by one, to the safety of the bank and the open arms of Velana and the rest of the party.

As they carried the last child, a little girl, across the ever-widening rushing stream of water, and placed her in Velana's arms, Miguel got caught up with some debris and was struggling to keep afloat. Ian turned and swam out to reach him, but they were both swept away by the fierce current and vanished under the churning white water. Velana was yelling their names but it was like a silent scream, as it was impossible for her to be heard above the screaming hurricane.

Pedro desperately ran along the crumbling bank to try and catch sight of the two men, but he knew in his heart that no one could survive in that boiling wall of water that was sweeping away towards the town and the sea beyond.

There was no hope for Ian and Miguel – they were gone forever. Pedro slowly bowed his head and blessed himself before turning towards the women and children who were struggling to get up to the relative safety of the mine shaft. The sky seemed to get even darker, heavy rain lashed at them and drenched the landscape as they finally made it to the mine opening. The eddying wind sucked inward, tearing at them; the heavy rain ran in rivulets underfoot, splattering against the opening, running down the mine shaft walls, soaking the dusty earth.

The wind shrieked and boomed at the mine's entrance, like a battery of guns going off with unnerving vehemence. Once inside the mine they lay down exhausted and huddled together to try and keep warm, as they were soaked to the skin.

Pedro did his best to make the tarpaulin into a larger tent shape so that he could get everyone under cover and protected from the draughty interior of the mine, all of the adults trying to soothe the children, who were whimpering and crying.

Pedro looked around and found an old storm lamp at the back of the mine, also some cooking utensils and a siram cooking kettle. He lit the lamp and filled the kettle up with water from the drips in the shaft and set it to boil with the aid of some bits of paper, sticks, and dry leaves.

The flickering glow from the lamp made his kneeling shadow dance grotesquely upon the roughly hewn walls as he crouched over the kettle. When the water was boiling, he broke up some bars of chocolate that he had in his pocket and made a kind of chocolate drink that tasted good and uplifting. This he passed round the children, some of whom were numb with fear as they hid under the tarpaulin. It was a welcoming drink and stopped them whimpering for the moment.

Velana held the twins to her breast and comforted them as best she could. They knew in their young minds that something terrible had happened to their grandpa, and that their happy day had suddenly become an unbelievable nightmare.

Heather was lying with her head in Maria's lap, both of them silently sobbing. Maria had lost her son, and Heather had lost her husband and her father; the two people she loved most were no longer with her, and she found it difficult to understand and grasp that fact. She kept calling out their names and begging for them to please come back to her and the brokenhearted Maria tried to console her daughter-in-law by stroking her forehead and gently running her fingers through her curly fair hair.

Towards late evening, the shriek of the typhoon was the only sound still raging outside; the children were starting to fall asleep, while the adults sat with almost identical expressions of shock and hopelessness on their faces.

Pedro crouched over the siram kettle for a little warmth, silent and unmoving. He thought of his father, Miguel, and wondered how he had fared back at the farm. He had stayed behind to look after the animals and Pedro suddenly feared the storm less than he feared what he'd find outside. He wondered if Father Silvas was safe and had survived the deluge that surely must have wrecked the little town.

He took Kirsty's hand; she was holding four sleeping children in her arms; her eyes met those of her husband, and her despairing expression slowly changed to one of thankfulness as she realised they still had each other and could face anything as long as they were together.

Pedro relaxed and fell into a deep sleep with his head leaning forward and his shoulders drooping, still clutching Kirsty's hand while, outside, the storm raged unabated.

Around five-thirty in the morning, just before daybreak, Theresa got up and went forward to the entrance of the mine shaft to look outside, sighing and mumbling to herself as she did so. In all the years she had lived here she had never experienced anything like this and she felt as though the world was coming to an end. To make matters worse, the storm showed no sign of diminishing: the rain lashed her face; she could taste the salt from the sea on her lips.

Kneeling down she prayed with all her heart that it would soon be all over for the sake of the children. The savagery outside made her begin to doubt if it would ever end but eventually the sky brightened as the first lull came, slowly blowing itself out after eighteen hours of terrible violence, though the high winds still continued for a few more hours, lessening their force until the tail end of the storm evaporated completely and all was silent.

Chapter Twenty-eight

The afternoon sun was trying to break through the dust-clouded sky as the bedraggled party emerged from the mine shaft, dazed and forlorn but ready to face the worst. Iona had a deep gash on her leg and was limping badly. Heather and Collette went to her aid and supported her as Pedro led them down the valley towards the town. Not one tree was left standing; there wasn't a roof spar or tile left anywhere in sight. As they approached the town they realised that the church and steeple had survived, together with some of the more strongly built houses in the main street.

Almost half the population had been killed or seriously injured and people were wailing and crying as they discovered that loved ones had been found dead among the rubble of flattened houses. Father Silvas was standing at the entrance to the church, calling out orders and directing the rescue parties into smaller groups.

Everyone admired his tough spirit and followed his instructions as he gave them all work to do. The church was improvising as a hospital to treat the injured, and a mortuary for the dead, where identification could begin. Burials would take place almost immediately in the graves that were being prepared in a field next to the churchyard cemetery. Father Silvas knew they would have to be buried as soon as possible as the bodies would decompose quickly in the hot climate.

He sat in his little battery car and drove down what was left of the main street, giving out orders. Some of the townspeople were kneeling and crouching on the ground, shattered and mindless with shock and disbelief.

"Go!" Father Silvas roared at them. "Help with the rescue! Round up everyone you can find and bring them here, and if you find any children alone and without parents, bring them also."

He went on to tell the women to boil water and make large pots of soup for the survivors. His voice was the only one to be heard among the townspeople who were stunned into silence as they went about their tasks, blindly following the directions of their trusted priest. He might be a man getting on in years but he was a true leader and no one thought to disobey him as they all gathered at the church to assist in the emergency rescue service.

Dr Valdez was one of the survivors and was already at work operating on some of the more seriously injured – using the top of a door laid across the pews in the church – quietly getting on with the task of stitching up wounds, now and again calling for more hot water and disinfectant.

Everybody had sprung into action, even the children had organised themselves into a little human chain and were passing buckets of water from the nearby, now subsiding, River Ola. The old stone bridge that spanned the river had collapsed and was lying in a heap of rubble, like some dead dinosaur of long ago.

Velana suddenly had thoughts of Jose, and how they had made wonderful love under the arches of the bridge all those years ago. So much had happened in between; she felt the need of his strength now and wondered what his life was like and if she would ever see him again.

Pedro was helping to carry people into the church, one of them a woman whose legs had been badly mangled. Dr Valdez opened her blouse and discovered her chest was also crushed and he marvelled that she had managed to hang on this long. But he knew the spirit of the townspeople; this woman had struggled hard to survive and she simply didn't know how to lie down and die. He prepared a painkilling injection for her, and as he held her hand, she moved her fingers slightly, gave a sigh, and relinquished her spirit to the Almighty. Dr Valdez stroked her forehead and gently closed her eyes, sighing himself with weariness and sadness as he signalled for the next patient to be brought in.

Theresa expressed a wish to go home to see how much damage had been done, and Maria wanted to see how Miguel senior was and if he'd made it through the earthquake and storm. Pedro and Velana offered to come with them, surprised when they got there to discover how little damage had been done to both properties, except for a few broken windows, dislodged roof tiles, and the odd fallen tree.

The farms were situated in a sheltered valley, which explained why they had missed the main force of the storm, but Miguel senior had not escaped unharmed; he had injured his foot and was hobbling around with a makeshift crutch when Maria arrived. They looked at one another, their faces lighting up, but it was a short-lived joy. She took him in her arms and broke the sad news about Ian and Miguel and how they had saved the children at the cost of their own lives, and they cried together for their son and for Heather, left so prematurely widowed.

After checking that no other damage had been done at the Domingo farm, Theresa, Velana, and Pedro made their way back down the valley to the town. There was work to be done at the church; more and more people were arriving, some being supported by others more able than themselves, some on makeshift stretchers, all of them needing help in these traumatic moments of their lives.

It was heart-rending watching it all but there was no time for anyone to sit still and do nothing. Gradually people stopped crying and tried to assist in any way they could, even as they strove to grasp the situation as it was and the way things had been before disaster struck at their community.

The rescue forces and nursing teams worked like demons to free the last of the people who were still trapped in their wrecked homes, the comradeship and everyone pulling together keeping the nurses alert and busy while the salvage crews sweated and strained at fallen masonry and heavy timbers.

Chapter Twenty-nine

The next few days saw outside help arriving from nearby Faro – doctors and firemen and some heavy lifting equipment to clear the flattened houses. It was painstaking work and sniffer dogs were brought in to try and locate survivors though, by the time they got some of them out, they were usually beyond help.

Services for the dead were held every day, and the terrible moment came when two bodies that were found trapped under some tree roots further down the valley, were identified as Ian and Miguel, Ian clutching Miguel as if he had been trying to save him.

Both of them had died as heroes; that's what Father Silvas said in his sermon at the open air service as the men were laid to rest, a congregation of hundreds praying for their souls, including Jose, who had arrived and was assisting Father Silvas.

Velana, brokenhearted at the loss of her father, nevertheless kept her emotions in control as she and the other members of her family supported Heather, who was grieving sorely for her husband as well as her father.

But when Velana saw Jose, dressed in his purple robes, older looking – a little bald patch on the top of his head, a distinguished greying at his temples – it was all too much for her and she broke down and sobbed her heart out.

Theresa took her daughter into her arms and held her

close as her whole body shook with emotion, and the twins, worried by the sight of their mother's grief, went to her and offered comfort, Edward looking up at her and saying, "Don't cry, Mamma, we're here and we love you."

Velana wiped her eyes and gazed down into his deep blue eyes. In them she saw a reflection of the strength that had been in their father and grandfather, and the conviction grew in her that the spirits of both men were still here and would go on living within those they had left behind. A surge of wondrous hope swelled in her breast at the thought; she held her head high, and lifting up her children she joined in the singing of the Portuguese and Scottish version of 'Abide with Me'.

After the service, Velana spoke briefly with Jose. He took her hand and said, "How are you, Velana? You're looking well and haven't changed a bit since I last saw you. It must be seven years now . . . and these must be the twins I've heard so much about." Placing a hand on each little head he whispered, "God bless you, my children," to which they both answered at the same time, "Pleased to meet you, Father," and smiled up at him.

Velana looked into his dark eyes and whispered, "Should I call you Father Jose, now that you are a priest?" She felt a little nervous and tense speaking to him after all these years; sad also, knowing that their lives had taken such different paths after all that they had meant to one another.

"No, just call me Jose, as you always did; we are friends forever, remember?"

Velana noticed a warm twinkle in his eyes as he spoke. She felt weak at the knees and a strange choking feeling arose at the back of her throat. It was still there, that loving feeling for him after all these years. She couldn't help herself; she knew that he was untouchable, but that didn't stop her heart reaching out to him. She wanted to take him in her arms and hold him, to tell him how she felt, but for them that was impossible, and so much had happened since last they had held each other so long ago.

He seemed to sense the tension in her and murmured, "My famous Velana, you have done so much with your life. Did you know that I've got every one of your recordings? I once saw you in Paris, at one of your concerts, but there were thousands of fans and I couldn't get near you. But it was wonderful to see you and hear you sing. You sounded so professional and confident. I felt so proud of you."

"Oh, it's just like any job, you get good at it if you work hard enough – as I'm sure you know yourself." She tried to sound offhand but the words came out stilted and unnatural.

Guida, who was standing nearby, sensed the awkwardness of the situation and broke into the conversation. "It's true, no one works harder than our very special Velana." She extended her hand and smiled at him. "Pleased to meet you, Father, my name is Guida and I'm Velana's musical adviser."

Velana was glad of the interruption; she began to feel more at ease, but it was too late – some of the other mourners wanted to speak to Jose. He glanced briefly into Velana's eyes and whispered, "Please excuse me, I would have loved more time with you . . ." Abruptly he turned away from her and went to mingle with the crowd.

Velana watched him, her eyes growing misty – he would always be her guiding star, her knight in shining armour . . .

"Come on." Guida took her hand and pulled her

away, saying, "He really is a handsome man but he belongs to the church now. Everybody loves him as they would love God and His teachings but we have to get on with life and try to help others as best we can. I think the one that's needing our help right now is poor Heather, she looks devastated."

Velana realised how right she was and said gratefully, "What would I ever do without you, Guida? You always say the right things and come up with the right answers."

Guida smiled. "That's what friends are for, as I've told you often enough before."

Taking Eva and Edward by the hand she led them over to where their Aunt Heather stood, lost and forlorn-looking, but smiling a little when she saw the bright rosy faces of her niece and nephew, always lightening any situation with their childish chatter and carefree laughter.

Then came the rain, a warm, wind-blown drizzle sweeping across the valley, as though the heavens were weeping with the mourners over the fresh graves of those who had been lost.

Father Silvas was praying over the last person to be buried that day, and as he led the congregation in reciting the rosary, the warm, light tears of rain fell from the kingdom of heaven, and continued to fall, even after everyone had dispersed and made their way back to what was left of their town, to start building anew in days to come and hopefully taking fresh heart.

The earthquake had only lasted a few minutes but the aftermath of both it and the storm left devastation stretching all along the southern coast of Portugal.

Huge sections of mountainous cliffs had fallen into the turbulent sea; coastal waterside villages had been swept away by the giant tidal waves, and larger towns like Faro and Lagos had been badly damaged.

The effects of the hurricane were felt all over the world. One of the largest waves reached the Channel Islands and Great Britain, causing severe flooding in low-lying areas, and even reaching the American coast on the other side of the Atlantic, the following day.

The rebuilding of the worst-hit areas would take years to achieve but the Portuguese people had always been resilient and hard-working, and within a few weeks the airport at Faro was reopened and outside aid was being flown in.

Velana and Collette had soon realised that they could help to make a lot of money by running charity concerts all over Europe, in an effort to sustain the victims and their families. Velana also knew that long-term employment was what was needed for the young people of Olhão. There had always been farming and fruit growing but there weren't enough jobs to go round, and the majority of young people had to move away from home to find work elsewhere.

She loved her little town and its people and wanted to see it thrive again. She felt the same way about Corrish and the other Scottish islands. Iona had said the same situation of unemployment existed there, with youngsters having to leave home to find jobs.

Velana felt a deep need to go back to Corrish, for that was the place where she got the most inspiration for her songs and music.

She, Iona, and Guida worked well together and so it was decided, at the end of their exhausting tour of all the major cities, to make their way back to Corrish for a springtime vacation.

Even Theresa came. She had never flown in a plane before and found it quite daunting, though she tried her best not to show it, especially to the twins, as she would do anything to be near them and wanted to be close to them at all times, more so since their terrible experience during the earthquake.

The helicopter gave a slight bump as it touched down near the McKinnon croft. Theresa hastily blessed herself and felt relieved at being back on the ground.

To Iona, this was a particularly sad homecoming. She had travelled all over the world and seen a lot of places, but this was her home; here she had been brought up along with her two sisters who were now far away in Portugal. She felt that her father should be here to welcome her, as he had always been in bygone days when she had come home for the long school holidays. But he was dead now, that big, fair giant of a man with his eyes crinkling in the sun and his long legs taking him swiftly to meet her, no matter how long or how short a spell she'd been away.

She would never see him here again, on his beloved island, and her heart felt sad and empty as she stood there surveying the places he had walked . . . remembering how he had smiled and laughed . . .

"Come on," Collette was there by her side, taking her hand, hugging her close in that special way that was so comforting.

As the noise of the helicopter engines faded, the sound of barking excitedly filled the air and Bracken came bounding to meet everyone, still sound of wind and limb although he was getting on in years. He loved company, and when he saw the twins he yelped with joy and did a little hop and dance around them. They had been quite small on their last visit, but he remembered them and squealed with delight when they threw their arms around his neck and cuddled him, thereafter making sure he didn't let them out of his sight when they ran off to reacquaint themselves with their surroundings.

Ian's cousin, Alex McPhee, and his wife, had looked after everything well and the place was shining like a new pin. Alex was there at the door to welcome everybody as they went inside, doffing his cap in a most polite manner and saying in his clear, island voice, "Welcome home, girls, Morag and me have done our best to look after the croft in your absence and we were devastated to hear the sad news about your father. He was a great man and he'll be missed by many of the islanders. He was always helping others, whether it was financial, or just a friendly word, and everyone in the community looked up to him."

Velana felt tears welling up in her eyes. Clearing her throat she whispered. "Thanks Alex, you and Morag have done a wonderful job keeping the place in order and, if its allright with you, we'd like both of you to stay on as housekeeper and overseer."

Alex's face lit up. "We'll be delighted to help in any way we can, our croft is only three fields away so we'll always be near at hand if you need us. So come away in, all of you, Morag has a pot of stew simmering on the stove and the table is all prepared."

Morag was a fat, jolly woman with apple-red cheeks; her whole body wobbled when she laughed, and when she spoke she gurgled, as if her mouth was full of water, but it was a happy sound which made people laugh with her.

Theresa took to her immediately; they had the same ideas on how to look after a farm and there was a strong similarity between the Portuguese and Hebridean ways of doing things which made Theresa feel instantly at home.

The meal was simple but delicious. Theresa complimented Morag on her wonderful cooking, especially her apple crumble. Morag expanded with pride, she gurgled, she beamed at Theresa and urged her to have second helpings. Theresa graciously accepted and everyone else followed suit, especially the twins, whose enormous appetites never seemed to diminish, no matter how much they had eaten.

Morag swung the big cast-iron kettle with the heavy chain over the peat fire; she pumped the leather bellows, coaxing the fire into life. The kettle began to whistle and spout steam and everyone was invited to partake of a nice cup of tea to wash down their dinner.

The twins asked to be excused and made a beeline for the back door with Bracken chasing at their heels in hot pursuit, delighted that he had some young people to play with at last, and he squealed with delight as the three of them ran along the garden path to explore the rest of the croft.

Chapter Thirty

Collette couldn't wait to get her paintbox out and after dinner, with another couple of hours of daylight left, she and Iona set off along the beach on a painting expedition.

Collette wanted to try and capture a Hebridean sunset in watercolour. She had been teaching Iona how to paint and it added a whole new dimension to the younger girl's talents. Collette said that she was a natural artist, and needed only to be shown the basic rudiments, as she already had an eye for composition and perspective.

Corrish was an artist's paradise, a landscape filled with sparkling, vivid colour, distant blue mountains and soaring peaks coming out of misty shadows to make an ethereal background for a painter's canvas.

As they walked along, the girls were captivated by the island's natural beauty; nothing disturbed the evening calm, the only sounds were that of nature: the lapping of the waves on the shell sand beach; the call of the sea birds from the nearby cliffs. The evening sky was primrose-yellow under low-slung purple clouds; small groups of sheep cast dark shadows on the twilight machair, and the feeling of life was all around as the evening light overflowed into clouds of gold and the sea was flooded with a liquid, fiery glow.

Both Collette and Iona held their breaths as they delicately applied paint to paper, trying to capture the ever-changing scene. The shadows were growing longer and the tones getting deeper till the cliffs and the distant islands were in silhouette against a honey-gold sky.

"There, it's done," Collette decided at last. "That will do us for tonight, we can come back tomorrow and do any finishing touches that might need doing."

Iona felt contented and relaxed as they packed up their gear. In the semi-darkness they happily made their way hand in hand along the beach and back towards the house.

"I wish we could stay here on this island, forever," Collette murmured. "It's so beautiful, it's the sort of place where love is born and we could be together always."

"Oh, Collette," said Iona shakily, "I feel the very same way. Although I was brought up on the island I have never taken it for granted and I have always felt a deep love for the place, even more now that we are sharing it together."

Velana and Guida were also deeply inspired by the island's beauty but in a slightly different way. They both could draw their inspirations from the atmosphere and put it down in music. Velana would sing and hum her heartfelt melodies and Guida would work on the lyrics and arrangements. On their many rambles around the island they wrote about the spring flowers in the sunshine, the wild sea birds cry, the ever-changing sounds of the sea and the crystal clear island air; it was all music to their ears. Even the spring showers and droplets of rain were in harmony with the soft breezes blowing down through the glens from the mountains and the distant peaks.

They had been on the island about three weeks, and it was when they were on one of their hill walks, crossing over a rocky stream, that Guida fell and sprained her ankle. Velana bathed it with cool water from the stream but it was swelling pretty badly. "Come on, we'll have to get you home," Velana said briskly. "Put your arm round my neck and let me take most of your weight."

Guida didn't argue, she knew how determined Velana was. She clung to Velana and hobbled painfully along and slowly they made their way down over the moor. They hadn't gone very far when they both had to stop for a rest at an outcrop of rock.

"Can I be of assistance?" Both women jumped with fright when a manly voice from above addressed them. "I saw you crossing the moor and thought you might need some help." A tall figure appeared in front of them and added in a friendly voice, "My name is Craig Ferguson, in case you're wondering who I am, and I'd like to offer you my assistance."

"Oh, that's very kind of you." Velana quickly recovered from her surprise and with a smile she introduced Guida and herself and explained what had happened.

He glanced down at Guida's ankle. "That looks nasty. We'd better get you to the doctor in the village. My mountain jeep is parked just over the hill, let's get you over to it." And with one sweep of his powerful arms he lifted Guida up as though she was a feather pillow and carried her up the hill, saying over his shoulder to Velana, "Would you mind bringing my bag and field glasses? They're lying back there on top of that rock."

Velana collected the gear and followed him, admiring his strong physique and handsome features. He looked as though he was in his early thirties with dark, almost blue-black flowing hair. He walked proud, full of confidence, with a professional air about him, and when he smiled it was like a beam of sunshine.

He carried Guida up to the jeep and made her

comfortable in the front seat and Velana slipped in beside her.

"Hang on!" he cried as he started the engine and put it into gear and drove off at breakneck speed down through the bumpy glen terrain. Velana enquired if he was here on holiday.

"No, I work here. I'm a research chemist and I'll be here for a few months. I'm doing a survey of the plant life on Corrish and there are some quite unusual species, especially on the higher ground; that is why I was up here today."

"Lucky for us," Guida said ruefully as she rubbed her painfully-swollen ankle.

Craig smiled at Velana and said, "I'm sure I've seen you some place before but I don't know where. Have we met at any time?"

"No, I don't think so." Velana's eyes sparkled. "I certainly would have remembered you if we had ever crossed paths."

She gave her head a little shake and her long flowing blonde hair swirled around her shoulders. He glanced at her and grinned. "I've got it, you're the famous singer lady who's staying on the island. Velana Domingo. I've heard the villagers talking about you. Everybody loves and admires you."

He was shouting a little to make himself heard above the jeep's engine and, gripping the steering wheel, he slowed down slightly in an effort to drive more carefully, as if suddenly realising that he had important people on board and didn't want anything to happen to them. "Won't be long now," he told them, "the doctor's house is at the end of the village."

The doctor didn't take long with his diagnosis and advised Guida to have a complete rest for a week.

"That means I won't be able to go to the triple peaks with you tomorrow as planned," Guida told Velana in dismay as Craig carried her out of the surgery and sat her in the jeep.

"Well, if you could put up with me I could accompany you tomorrow," Craig suggested to Velana. "I've been meaning to go up there sometime so why not make it tomorrow?" He added with a smile, "Is it a date then?"

Velana nodded. "Yes, it's a date, on one condition."

"What's that?"

"That you let me help you with your research. I know quite a lot about plant life and we could maybe share a few ideas."

"That sounds wonderful." Craig sounded jubilant as he drove the jeep along the coast road towards the McKinnon croft.

Chapter Thirty-one

The twins came running across the field, with Bracken leading the way, as they caught sight of the jeep coming along the road and up to the croft.

"What's wrong with Auntie Guida?" Edward asked in a breathless, worried voice as Craig carried Guida up the path and into the house.

"She's sprained her ankle, but it'll be OK in a few days," Velana explained. "Nothing to get upset about."

She took Edward and Eva by the hand and followed Craig into the house where he had just lowered Guida gently into the armchair next to the fire. "There we are now, just take it easy and relax," he told her. "I'm sure these two young people will be only too glad to look after you." He smiled at the twins and said, "Hello, I'm Craig."

"Pleased to meet you, Sir." Edward returned in his most polite voice. "My name is Edward and this is my sister, Eva. This is Bracken, our dog."

Craig took Eva's hand and Bracken's paw. "I'm delighted to meet you all. How would you like to go for a ride in the mountain jeep?"

The twins' eyes lit up with excitement. They turned to Velana and cried out. "Oh, can we, Mamma? Please, please, please!"

"Yes, as long as you both behave and get strapped in."

Guida thanked Craig for all his help. "I don't know what we would have done without you today," she said with a yawn, as the effects of the doctor's sedative began to take hold.

"I was in the right place at the right time, that's all, and I was glad to be of help," he assured her warmly, and turning to the twins he cried, "right then, twice round the field, outside, at the double!"

The children giggled as he led the way outside, lifted them into the jeep, and strapped them in at the front while, Bracken – determined to go with them – settled himself in the back.

"Here we go! Hold on tight!" Putting the engine into gear, he pressed the accelerater and they were off across the bumpy field at fifty miles per hour, all four wheels off the ground at one point, landing back with a heavy thud to the delighted squeals of laughter from Edward and Eva and the surprised look on Bracken's face as he tried to keep his balance on a machine that seemed at times to be flying.

Velana watched them go round and round the field; it was so good to see the children enjoying themselves so much and she was glad that they had warmed towards Craig. Already she admired him a lot and felt really at ease with him.

A few minutes later they were all back at the house, Craig shouting, "Right, everybody off." Bracken was the first to jump down, happy to be on firm ground again; the children followed, flushed and excited, clamouring to thank Craig and ask him if they could do it again sometime.

"Any time, kids, I'm at your disposal. But, for now, I've got to get back. I've some work to finish off so I'll see you tomorrow morning." He caught Velana's eye and taking her hand he whispered, "I'm looking forward to our trek, I'll call for you early, around seven-thirty. Is that OK?"

"That will be fine, I'll be ready," said Velana. "I'll make a picnic lunch." He nodded and drove off down the road.

For the first time in ages, Velana felt warm and happy inside. As she turned to go into the croft, two bullfinches, a cock and a hen, were sitting on the windowsill preening each other and putting their beaks together, like some lovers' kiss, in the evening light. Digging in her haversack for some leftover breadcrumbs she held them out. Both birds jumped onto her outstretched fingers and began pecking at the crumbs, making little muffled warbling noises as they did so. Velana was surprised at how tame they were and utterly captivated as they began opening and closing their wings around her hand, seeming to sense that she was a country person who knew about wild things. She wanted to share the moment with the twins but was afraid to call out in case she startled the little creatures. Instead, she blew gently onto their feathers and started to sing to them.

> *"Meet me tonight in dreamland*
> *under the silvery moon,*
> *Meet me tonight in dreamland*
> *where the sweet roses bloom."*

It was a magical moment as her beautiful voice echoed around the garden, with the bullfinches whistling and unafraid, in harmony with her and her music.

Theresa and Morag, who were working in the kitchen, stopped what they were doing to listen to the wonderful sound of Velana and the birds singing. Guida could hear them clearly as she sat at the fireside, and switching on the tape recorder she got it all down on tape.

Outside, there was hardly a breath of wind to stir the grasses as Velana finished singing. The birds hovered around for a moment or two then flew off across the fields, weaving in and out of the hedgerows, leaving behind the magic of their little moment in the thoughts of all who had witnessed it, most especially Velana.

"We've just to cross the river and up on to the valley floor and we'll be there." Craig spoke loudly to Velana above the noise of the engine. They had been driving steadily up over the moor for about an hour and it was the first time Velana had been as high as this anywhere on the island. There were thick pockets of mist floating down from the summit, like gossamer veils swirling in ribbons that felt cool on Velana's face. Then slowly it cleared, and the bright blue sky appeared above the valley and over the triple peaks that were the landmarks of Corrish.

"It's going to be a lovely day," Craig declared with conviction. "Fill your lungs with that wonderful clear air, every breath is worth a fortune in the bank of health." Both of them took huge gulps, letting go of it slowly and steadily. "Pure nectar." Craig murmured appreciatively. "I wish we could bottle it and take it home with us."

A flood of silver light spilled over a small loch that lay in the middle of the valley, catching the rugged towers of the cliff-faces, turning the fading mist into an almost lilac colour. The loch was the same shade, tinged with a suggestion of golden yellow, copper-coloured near the shore, contrasting against the dark green velvet of the pine trees in the distance.

Velana was quite moved by the rich and vivid hues

and whispered, "This is a painter's paradise; I know Collette and Iona would just love to be here."

"They can come up any time; we'll be here for a few days yet." Craig drew up beside the loch as he spoke and started to unload his gear and equipment from the jeep. "I've got a lot of research to do on the local plant life, mainly for health and skincare treatments."

Velana was a willing worker and it wasn't long before she was helping Craig identify some of the different species of plants. With the aid of a syringe, he drew some of the liquid and sap from each plant without damaging it, afterwards mixing them together in little phials and testing them in his makeshift laboratory.

Among other things, this contained a little still, to aid him in the distillation process for wild lavender and other plants that had to be distilled immediately after picking.

"Amazing," Craig said as they continued testing. "A lot of these plants can be used in skincare treatments and aromatherapy, and most of them only grow in this valley. I'm delighted." Excitedly he turned to Velana, and taking her hand he pulled her towards him and put his arms around her. "Velana," he whispered, "I'm so happy that we're together like this, and, if it's not too soon to say it, I'd love if we could go on being this way for always."

And they kissed. A long, lingering kiss, holding each other in a lover's embrace for what seemed like an eternity.

Velana could feel the strength in Craig's body and it felt wonderful to be close to him. "I feel the same way, Craig," she whispered huskily as their bodies melted together. She could hear the cry of an eagle in the distance, high above the peaks, echoing over the valley. And suddenly she pulled away from him. She wanted him, oh, how she wanted him, but not like this, not in the middle of his work and his research, knowing how important it was to him . . . the time wasn't yet right.

He looked into her eyes and whispered, "I understand, my darling, and I wouldn't do anything to hurt you, but I know in my heart that I love you. I've known that ever since I set eyes on you."

"But you hardly know me," Velana protested. "We've only just met."

"Have you ever heard of love at first sight?" His face was serious as he asked the question. "Well, that's what's happened to me, and I want to be close to you and to share in your life for the rest of my days . . . But for now . . ." he put his hand on her shoulder and said firmly, "let's have some lunch and then we can get back to work."

Velana was glad of the interruption, it helped her get her breath back and pull her thoughts together. Her head was buzzing at the things Craig had said to her. She felt flattered, and was attracted to him, but she also felt that events were moving a bit too fast and knew that she needed to think everything over and put it all in its proper perspective.

"Lunch is ready," she said, smiling as she handed him a tray with coffee and sandwiches. Both of them ate in silence for a while, then Velana whispered in low tones, "You know, I think that wild flowers and plants always look happier than cultivated blooms. Maybe it's because they get to choose their own spot in the landscape."

"What a wonderful thing to say." He gazed at her admiringly. "I know exactly what you mean. In my view, people who live in the country are much happier than people who live in the city, they can choose their spot in the wide open spaces and be with their true selves. That's exactly how I feel at the moment, because you are here with me in this wonderful place."

Chapter Thirty-two

Velana cleaned up the picnic dishes, then started to help Craig with more samples; he had found a rare plant called a sundew and he said quietly, "This is most unusual. The only other place this plant grows is on the Scottish mainland, near Loch Awe, but this sample is slightly different, it's a kind of insect catcher or flytrap – see the little folding leaves with sticky teeth on them? Once these leaves close like a little cage, it's goodbye Mr Fly."

"That would be a good plant for the croft," said Velana, "there are always plenty of bluebottles about, but elder leaves in a vase usually keep them away from the kitchen, and that includes midges and other flying pests."

"Yes, I've been researching and trying to find cream for ageing skin, and the elder plant is one of the ingredients I've been working with. But its all experimental at the moment and a lot more tests need to be done with other plants before I find the right concoction. I'm sure I will find it, though, maybe even on this island."

As they both searched for further samples, Velana noticed a bush that grew profusely all over the valley. It reminded her of the arbutus bush that flourished in Portugal; it was almost identical to the plant that was used in the making of the local brew, medronho, and even had the same type of blossom.

It was then that she told Craig how she and her father had distilled and produced the golden liquid that was so popular in the towns and villages of the Algarve.

"It's a secret process, one handed down through generations of families that have lived in the area. It's all to do with the type of copper still that is used; it has to easily control the temperature at different levels of the procedure and maintain the flow of the spirit."

Craig was surprised and delighted by the fact that she knew so much about the distilling process.

"Maybe we can put our heads together and come up with some new essential oils," he said, smiling at her. "That fruit plant you talked about, the arbutus, is related to the wild raspberry that grows on the Scottish mainland. The locals make jams, jellies, and wine from the flower and the fruit, but mostly through fermentation; they don't distill it in any way. At least, they aren't supposed to, it's against the law of the land to use a still to make any kind of alcohol . . . Except if you're a chemist like me," he added.

"That's a strange law," said Velana. "In Portugal you buy a still from the local coppersmith and its use is looked upon as harvesting nature's bounty. In no way is the law broken."

"Different countries, different laws," said Craig, "but I'd love to try your medronho sometime. I bet it has a real kick."

"It's a bit like Scottish whisky, and it's said to be good for the constitution," Velana told him with a laugh. "I think there are a couple of bottles in the croft; I'll let you have a taste some evening."

"Is that a promise?" said Craig as he looked into her face. She swept her hair over her shoulder and stood erect beside him, a tall, golden goddess of a girl with eyes that reflected the blue of the sky and skin that was smooth and creamy white.

"Yes, that's a promise," she whispered, and turned away from the expression of desire she saw deep in his eyes.

As the late afternoon sun began to cast long shadows over the valley floor, both Craig and Velana agreed it was time to pack up for the day.

"We can leave some of the gear," Craig decided, "it should be quite safe up here. Tomorrow, I'll bring a couple of tents so we'll be under cover if the weather breaks at any time."

They got into the jeep and headed down the valley, through the rich shades of brown, orange, yellow, and green, every now and then catching flickering glimpses of the silver waters of the loch through the trees, while above them, the towering peaks cast their sullen shadows.

As they stopped for a moment before crossing the river, Velana looked back. "This is truly a secret paradise," she said softly. "I'm glad we came and I want to thank you for a wonderful day." She took his hand and squeezed it and he responded by leaning over and kissing her very gently on the cheek.

The days of trekking up and down the valley led into weeks for Craig and Velana. He was very serious about his work, experimenting and cataloguing all the different samples, and she was delighted that she could help and assist him. It was so different from her singing career, and she had a secret longing to do this type of work full-time so that she wouldn't have to go back on the road and could spend more time with her mother and the twins.

Collette and Iona had also visited the valley and

thought it was a wonderful place to paint, the colours were so rich and sharp and ever-changing. Iona was becoming quite professional in her attitude to art, thanks to Collette's teaching and guidance. Both of them would paint continuously, producing some wonderful watercolours of the valley and the surrounding hills, pictures that would grace any art gallery in the country.

They were on one of these painting excursions, farther up the valley, sitting quietly sketching, when they heard Craig yelling and shouting happily at the top of this voice.

"We've got it! After all these months, we've finally got it!" He was holding onto Velana, dancing and prancing with her round the camp area. "This is the breakthrough we've been working for all this time," he breathlessly told her. "And it's all so simple, it's been staring us in the face all along. Thanks to you, my wonderful lady, we've got our skin elixir. The tests have proved positive, and it's your method of distilling the flowers that has been most successful."

Velana was delighted that she had helped him make the breakthrough after the long hours of hard work, testing, experimenting, and discarding, over and over again, until sometimes it had all seemed so fruitless. Often Craig had been in despair, but she had driven him on with her strong spirit, knowing within herself that they would eventually find success by mixing the old ways with the new.

"All we've got to do now is to find some backers on the mainland and put the elixir into production," he spoke excitedly as Collette and Iona came running into the camp to find out what was going on. The look on the faces of Craig and Velana said it all, they were laughing and crying at the same time, their eyes sparkling with the joy of their discovery. Collette and Iona congratulated them and suggested having a celebration.

"Do you mind if we borrow the jeep?" Collette asked. "I've got a bottle of champagne at the croft that's been waiting for a moment like this."

"Help yourself, but mind the bumps. Bring the kids back with you and raid the larder for lemonade and ice cream and anything else you can think of for a camp party."

Chapter Thirty-three

The jeep roared away. Velana watched it go, then turning to Craig she took his hand and said softly, "They'll be gone for at least a couple of hours. The sun is still high and hot – let's have a swim in the loch to freshen up."

She led him down to a rocky outcrop jutting out into the loch, forming a horseshoe-shaped sheltered bay, bordered by beech trees whose graceful spreading branches, and leaves of pale gold, made their own light and reflections in the still, dark pool below, giving the whole scene a touch of fairy-tale beauty.

Velana undid the buttons of her cotton dress, then with a quick movement she discarded her underclothes, standing proudly naked in front of Craig for a moment before turning and diving headlong into the cool waters of the loch.

She surfaced about twenty yards off shore and called on him to come in, but he was standing motionless where she had left him, mesmerised by the vision of Velana's beautiful body. He had never ever seen anyone quite like her and his fingers were all thumbs as he raggedly discarded his clothes and plunged into the water. With a few short strokes he was beside her, holding her, their bodies merging together like two enamoured dolphins as they swirled and dived as one.

He repeated her name over and over, telling her how

much he loved her, putting his strong hands around her waist to raise her head and shoulders above the water so that he could kiss her soft full breasts. She shuddered with delight as his lips brushed her erect, pink nipples.

"I want you to love me," she whispered, "I think you've been very, very patient, waiting this long."

They made their way out of the water. Gathering her into his arms he carried her up the dry mossy bank and laid her down on a soft carpet of wild flowers and grasses. Pulling his head down she kissed him full on the lips, a long, lingering kiss full of passion, feeling as though she could devour him, this strong, powerful man who loved her so.

When he kissed her back his mouth was gentle, but soon it deepened into something more, charging both their desires. She felt his hand on the small of her back, pulling her against his naked chest, and the brush of heated flesh on flesh drove her to a pitch of longing.

The woolly carpet of hairs on his chest felt rough against her creamy breasts and she gasped at the sensation of her proud, pink nipples pressing against him as his burning lips followed the contours of her face, and neck, and down the valley between her breasts, making her whole body come alive to his touch.

Loving, cherishing, possessive – his demanding kisses sent rivers of excitement flowing deep within her, churning them into a flooding turmoil that had been lying stagnant for too long. And finally, the banks were bursting, overflowing, sweeping her to the ultimate fulfilment.

She cried aloud and uncontrollably in her passion as dazzling lights exploded behind her eyes and a deafening sound filled her ears, like surf breaking on some wondrous secret shore.

And this powerful, masterful man had taken her there,

so ardently yet so lovingly, to a place where the ground had seemed to be moving and a volcano had erupted inside her.

"There is no escape for you now, my darling," he said in triumph, yet there was tenderness in his voice too. "You are mine forever."

The stag-like, musky scent of him, was in her nostrils. She loved the comfort of having him near her. With lazy fingers he lifted the blonde curtain of hair on her shoulders and brushed his lips against the soft, tingling skin of her neck.

Smiling up at him she laid her cheek against his and they lay there for a long time, their bodies entwined and clinging together in warm, deep contentment.

Then slowly they became aware of their surroundings in the woodland glade. A cool breeze blowing through the trees felt pleasant on their naked bodies. Velana nestled her head in Craig's arms while they talked and murmured gentle endearments, going over the magic they had shared.

"My darling Craig, you are a wonderful lover," she whispered, "I've never met anyone quite like you, you make me feel alive and special."

Craig didn't answer that; instead he said softly, "Velana, will you marry me? I love you so much and I know you love me, we're so natural together and I want to take care of you and the twins and for us all to be a family. You don't have to give me an answer just yet but please give it some thought. It's a serious business, talking about marriage," he added, his smile, like a cupid's arrow, going straight to her heart.

She was overjoyed at his proposal. "I can't think of anyone else in the whole wide world I'd rather marry than you, my darling, but let's give it some time and space, and logical thought first. We have our future project to consider. I've some ideas I'd like to put to you and even if we don't marry we can still be long-term partners – forever, if you like."

He nodded, "Allright, that's enough to be going on with, though I warn you, I'll give you no peace till you say you're going to be mine – all legal and binding."

He rose and stretched contentedly and she sighed at the sight of his beautiful frame, so tall and handsome and strong, and for a few moments she languished in luxurious thoughts of the joys they had just shared. But he was anxious in case the others came back, and gathering up her clothes he handed them to her and they both dressed rapidly . . . just in time. The jeep was coming up the valley, filling the air with its noisy intrusion. Craig and Velana looked at one another but before they headed back to the camp site their lips met in a long, lingering kiss.

Edward and Eva came running up to Velana, calling, "Are we going to have a party, Mamma? Auntie Guida has boxes of ice cream and lemonade in the jeep."

"Cakes and cookies too," added Eva, smiling happily at the thought of all the goodies.

"Yes, we're going to have a picnic party," said Velana, "you can both help set the table."

Jubilantly they ran off towards the jeep, with Bracken bounding at Edward's side as if he was tied to his foot. Every move Edward made, Bracken made too, displaying a rapport with the boy that was quite uncanny.

Soon everything was prepared and Velana asked everyone to gather round. Theresa, Guida, Collette and Iona, Eva and Edward, even Morag and Alex had managed to come. The champagne glasses were filled and Velana cried, "I'd like to propose a toast to Craig for his hard work and wonderful achievement, an achievement that could affect us all and everybody on the island. He wants to put his skin elixir into production and is looking for backers from the mainland. Well I, for one, want to back him every step of the way. Along with your support and hard work we could produce the elixir right here – our very own company on Corrish."

"That's a great idea," said Collette, "count me in. I can do your marketing. I've got a lot of experience in the business side of things."

"Sounds good," approved Craig, "but I want you all to be partners in this. We are in it together, and if we roll up our sleeves the elixir could be in production in roughly three to four weeks' time, but we'll have to find premises first."

"There's an old boatyard in Corrish that is for sale," Guida put in. "How would that do for a lab?"

"I know the one," Craig nodded. "It would do nicely. It could be converted into a lab quite easily and there's plenty of room for expansion."

Theresa, listening to all this, saw how happy and radiant Velana looked. It was a long time since she had seen that look on her daughter's face and guessed that she and Craig were lovers.

Theresa was glad for them and would go along with anything that would make the twins and their mother happy. They were her whole life and she wanted what was best for them. She looked at Craig and said, "Show us what to do and we'll help you all we can."

"Well, almost everything we will need is right here on the island, with the exception of some specimens and the things we'll have to import. After that, we'll be ready to go."

He smiled at Theresa, grateful for her enthusiasm, which he noticed was rubbing off on the rest of the little party. They were all chattering away, sharing ideas about the new project.

Iona for one was delighted; anything that would keep herself and Collette on their beloved island was allright with her. She had been born here and she belonged here. With the group, she had travelled and had seen the world; now it was time to settle down more and not go on the road as much as in the past. They could still do recording, maybe a tour every so often to keep the fans happy. In that way they could slowly ease off, though it was whatever Velana decided that mattered.

It soon transpired that everyone else was of the same mind; they were all willing to give Craig's proposals a try and Velana could see the potential of forming a company, for as well as the production of skin elixir, they could also concentrate on the growing market for essential oils used in aromatherapy and health and beauty treatments. Her dream of recruiting and employing local young people would be realised, part in Corrish, the other part in her own little town of Olhão, but first they would have to negotiate the purchase of land here on the island . . .

A tide of exhuberance rose in her. She raised her glass and cried, "Here's to our new company!"

"To our new company!" everyone echoed, but Collette interrupted the toast.

"We'll need a name that flows off the tongue easily and has a natural ring to it."

The twins were listening intently to the conversation and Eva said simply, "Why not call it Berry Bloom after all the little berries and flowers that Craig and Mamma have been working with?" She stood there with her big blue eyes, fair hair, chubby cheeks and little rosebud-cushion lips, looking so innocent and yet so wise.

There was a slight pause for a moment then Velana took Eva in her arms, proud of the fact that her little daughter had named the company. "That's it! That's it!" she enthused delightedly. "Its perfect. Here's to Berry Bloom Essential Oils."

"Berry Bloom Essential Oils!" they all repeated as they raised their glasses and cheered, and the happy sounds echoed round the valley.

Chapter Thirty-four

Beams of strong Portuguese sunlight flooded in through the windows of the waiting room of the new hospital, just off the main street of Olhão. Doctors and nurses and day patients were coming and going, toing and froing, in a hive of activity.

Velana was sitting in the waiting room glancing through some magazines, when Dr Valdez came in. "Father Silvas has had another slight stroke," he said sadly, "but he is a hardy old character, I'm sure he'll pull through. The nurses are working with him now. You will be able to see him in about thirty minutes; if you would like to wait you can use my office, it's much quieter there."

"Thank you Doctor, you've been so kind," Velana said as she followed him along the corridor. Stopping, he pointed his finger towards his office.

"Take a seat in there, the nurse will call you when she's ready. If you need a drink or anything just ask her."

Velana looked out of the window. The sun was very high in the deep blue sky, a soft, lazy breeze was blowing through the curtains, cooling her face. She settled down with her thoughts. Things had moved very quickly since she and the others had formed the company in Corrish, almost eighteen months ago. The production of the skin elixir and the essential oils had been an overnight success; the demand from all over the world was staggering and within six weeks most of the islanders were in full employment.

Collette and Iona had done a wonderful job with marketing and advertising – Collette had many contacts, some as far away as Japan and the Far East – but it was Velana's fame as an international star that had pushed things along and opened doors.

Craig had been working nonstop, urging everyone on, and he was delighted with the efforts of the islanders, though he had soon realised that expansion was needed to keep up the demand. And so they had opened up a branch factory here in Olhão and also one near Monchique in the high country of the Algarve, employing all the local people.

Theresa was delighted with the move back to Portugal and was happy to see her friends again. Maria and her husband, with the help of Pedro, Heather, and Kirsty, had done a wonderful job of looking after the farm while the Domingos had been away.

Kirsty had a little baby boy of her own now, he was the image of Pedro and they had named him Ian, after her father. Heather was still pretty devastated by what had happened to Miguel and Ian but was slowly coming to terms with it, gradually coming out of herself as she started to realise that life goes on, no matter what. She had poured her heart and soul into helping in the new venture 'Berry Bloom Essential Oils', and had never been busier.

Velana had all but given up her singing career, except for a few recordings of new songs with Iona and Guida, but as soon as each session was over with, it was straight back to work at the factory and lab.

She loved the camaraderie of family and friends, all

working together, and felt at ease and relaxed in the sweet-scented distilling areas of the laboratories. She also loved Craig dearly and when he begged her for the umpteenth time to marry him, she finally agreed. They decided to have the wedding here in Olhão, her home town, and they asked Father Silvas to perform the ceremony and bless the marriage.

So the plans for the biggest local wedding the townsfolk had ever seen, were set in motion. Craig wanted everybody to be there from the town and surrounding areas, and also from Corrish, where their love and their ideas for 'Berry Bloom' had taken seed and blossomed. He had no family of his own, both his parents were dead, but he had an old aunt who lived in the border country of Scotland where he was born, and he was delighted when he got the news that she was coming to the wedding to meet his beautiful bride.

The twins were all excited and talked nonstop about the coming event. Large marquees were set up to cater for the hundreds of guests and also for accommodation as there weren't that many hotels in Olhão to cope with the vast crowd.

But all that was far from Velana's mind as she sat in Doctor Valdez's office, waiting for the nurse to come and tell her how Father Silvas was. Just a short while ago he had been sitting in his beloved garden with herself and Craig, making last-minute plans for the wedding, which was to be the next day.

He was such a down-to-earth man of the world. Velana felt as though she could tell him anything, he had been there for her from the start of her life: he had baptized her; had given her first communion; he was there when she had been confirmed; and now he was going to marry her in the same church where all these events had taken place. He liked Craig and knew that they were suited to each other; it would be a good marriage and he would pray for them.

He had smiled at Velana and Craig and had started to rise off the garden bench but had suddenly fallen back, his head flopping to the side, his eyes half open and unmoving, a strange gurgling sound coming from his throat. Craig acted immediately, laying him on his side on the seat, undoing his collar, taking his pulse, whispering to Velana, "Quick, phone for an ambulance, he's unconscious."

The nurse came in to Dr Valdez's office and said, "We're all ready for you, Miss Domingo. You can see Father Silvas now." She led Velana to a little side room and whispered, "Try to keep him quiet. He needs complete rest."

Velana sat at the bedside and held the old priest's hand. He had the settled look of a man who wasn't going anywhere soon. She wondered if he was silently praying. He opened his eyes and saw Velana sitting at his bedside; she was wearing a simple white cotton dress with a flared pleated skirt and a pink, scented rose in her hair. She looked more lovely than he had ever imagined a girl could look and she reminded him of his beloved rose garden.

He raised his arm and ran his hand through his shock of silvery hair and tried to sit up, but she put her hands on his shoulders and laid him back on the pillow. His face was grey and clammy and he began to slip into semi-consciousness.

"Just feel weak," he whispered, "and a bit tired." He closed his eyes; his lids felt like two iron doors slamming shut, but just before he drifted off he mumbled "Get another priest to marry you, Velana. The wedding must go on, all the arrangements have been made." He could say no more; he started to breath heavily but evenly as finally he slept.

Velana tiptoed out of the room and quietly closed the door behind her.

Dr Valdez was waiting to speak to her. "He'll be like that for the next few days, in and out of consciousness, but all he talks about is you and how the wedding must go on. He doesn't want you to cancel for his sake. It's your big day and he wants to see you happy . . . as do I, Velana." He took her hand. "And I'm coming to the wedding. I wouldn't miss it for the world – now run along and get yourself prepared," he added, smiling.

"Thank you, Doctor, for everything," said Velana. "My mind is more settled now."

"I understand." He patted her hand. "See you in church."

Craig was waiting for her at the entrance to the hospital, he knew she was deeply upset by what had happened to Father Silvas and taking her in his arms he brushed her cheek with a delicate kiss. "I'll love and cherish you always, my sweetheart, and I know our marriage will be truly blessed. I've asked Maria to contact Jose and he's agreed to come all the way from France to marry us."

Velana felt a comforting flutter in her heart at the mention of Jose's name. She realised that this was fate. This was the way it was meant to be, and a person's life was all laid out in front of them, fitting together like a jigsaw. And now Jose, her childhood sweetheart, was coming back into her life to bless her marriage to Craig. She felt an inner glow flooding her body, as though she was floating on air, and she realised in her heart that all would be well as she pressed herself closer to Craig's loving embrace.

Chapter Thirty-five

Her wedding day dawned to a sunny and cloudless sky. Theresa was knocking on her bedroom door and entering with a laden tray in her hands. "I know it's early, but I want you to have a good breakfast before you start to get dressed. It's going to take you at least a couple of hours to fit in to all this finery."

Velana stretched her arms and said, "Oh, Mamma, how thoughtful of you, it's a long time since I had breakfast in bed." Aware of her mother's pride in her heritage, Velana had chosen to be married in traditional Portuguese Minhota-style regional dress, as that was where her grandmother had come from many years ago, before settling in the Algarve. As long as Velana could remember, a photograph of her had stood on top of Theresa's dressing table, showing her dressed in her traditional black wedding dress, encrusted in gold motifs, beads and trinkets. When Velana was a little girl, she had thought her grandmother had looked so regal, that she was the 'Queen of Portugal'. Velana had always wished that she could have a dress like that, and now, not only was her wish coming true, but her six bridesmaids would be dressed exactly the same.

After breakfast, Maria, Kirsty, and Heather arrived, joined soon afterwards by the hairdresser, the dressmaker and fitter, and a wave of excited bridal chatter echoed around the farm.

The sound resembled a cage full of budgies as they rushed from the farmhouse to the adjoining mobile homes and back to the farmhouse for the different fittings of their attire. Brimming with wedding day energy, they rushed in and out in a hub of feverish activity, pulling on the layers of stiff, starched petticoats on top of the pure white knitted stockings, followed by the beautiful black velvet dresses and the little black clogs on their feet.

Velana's long blonde hair was piled high on her head and supported with a small veil of lace and gold pins, traditionally borrowed from family and friends. Gold chains and brooches covered her dress, and around her neck she wore the beautiful heart-shaped pendant that Craig had given her as a wedding present, with the entwined initials VC inscribed in the centre.

Maria said, "Remember your flowers. I've prepared your garland posy with the candle in the centre." She placed it in Velana's hand as they all lined up for photographs to be taken outside the farmhouse before leaving for the church, Velana in the middle, surrounded by her bridesmaids, Collette, Iona, Guida, Kirsty and Heather, and little Eva, who looked like an old-fashioned doll in her period costume, standing beside her mother.

"You all look gorgeous," said the photographer as he clicked away with his camera before the cars arrived and whisked them off to be welcomed by the waiting crowds outside the church and more photographs before entering.

Edward was waiting to escort his mother down the aisle. He was immaculately dressed in a little black suit, white shirt, and purple bow tie. He face was beaming as he led Velana to the altar where Craig was standing beside Pedro, his best man, and Jose was waiting to join the couple in holy matrimony, witnessed by the packed congregation. The children's choir were singing 'Morning Has Broken' for the first hymn of the hour-long service which Jose conducted in a heart-warming, professional manner.

When he finally said the words, "Do you Velana, take Craig to be your lawful wedded husband?" she smiled at Jose, and turning she looked into Craig's loving eyes as she whispered, "I do."

"I pronounce you man and wife. In the name of the Father, and of the Son, and of the Holy Ghost. Amen." Jose made the sign of the cross, blessing them both, and then he whispered to Craig, "You may kiss the bride."

Craig looked adoringly at Velana and kissed her gently. Velana took his arm, and proudly he led her from the church. This was her special day and he wanted everyone to see his special bride.

Theresa and Maria were deeply moved by the ceremony, and tears of joy flowed down their cheeks as the bride and groom lined up for more photographs with the bridesmaids and bridal party, the colourful blue and purple bougainvillea that covered the church wall making a perfect background setting for the bridal scene.

The noise and bustle of wedding day excitement filled the bright morning, the crowd thronged and pushed to get a better view as the bride and groom, followed by the bridesmaids, paraded through the village in procession.

Velana looking radiant, and Craig spectacularly handsome, dressed in his dark-tailed morning suit, the bridesmaids walking with hands on their hips in traditional Minhota style and loving every minute of it, and smiles beaming on every face as the spectators showered the happy couple with flower petals and blessings.

The procession passed and moved on towards the tented reception area where Velana and Craig would receive their guests with kisses and congratulations and popping champagne corks, and after the wedding meal was over they would listen to the storytelling by the elderly father figures among the guests.

The magnetic sound of accordions and fiddles filled the air and the bandleader, announcing the first of the dances, beckoned everyone to be on the floor. First Velana and Craig, leading off with a modern waltz, dancing in perfect time to the music, revolving and weaving and gliding into reverse turns; moving as one.

"You look radiant, my darling," Craig whispered. "I want to hold you and dance with you forever; you're dancing divinely and feel as light as a feather."

"Only because I'm dancing with you, my wonderful man," Velana returned. Craig took a deep breath and pulled her closer to him as they moved along in the now crowded dance floor. The music changed, beating out a lively rhythm called the 'Ira', a quick-stepping country dance which consisted of intricate squares and patterns, the dancers yelling and screaming as they whirled and weaved in and out of each other's arms. Then they changed partners and danced the 'Malhao' which in turn, gave way to 'Caminha Verde', then the 'Chuba'.

"At last I can have a dance with the bride." Jose was suddenly there, standing in front of Velana after the last partner had changed. He had discarded his church robes and was wearing a smart dark suit. Without waiting for an answer he inclined his head a little, and taking Velana's hand he led her into the next dance.

"There's one thing for sure," Velana said a trifle breathlessly, "you haven't forgotten how to dance."

"I suppose it's a bit like riding a bike, once you've mastered it, you never forget how to do it," Jose smiled at her as they flowed smoothly across the floor to the beat of an old-fashioned waltz.

"Oh Jose, I am so rapturously happy," gasped Velana, "to have all my friends and loved ones around me at my wedding."

"You are a very special person," whispered Jose. "You are full of love and understanding, that is why everyone is here to give you their blessings, including me, most of all. We grew up together, we lived and loved and went down our separate roads. I have found peace and love and happiness in the church and you have found true love and happiness with Craig. We must have no regrets, it's all as it was meant to be."

Velana took his finger and kissed his ring; she did the same with the back of his hand. "Oh, Jose," she said huskily, "you always say the right thing. I am so proud that you were part of my life, in mind, body, and spirit."

"I'll always be your friend, Velana." His voice was soft and warm. "And if ever you need advice about anything you know where I'll be." The music stopped and he led Velana across the floor to where Craig was standing.

"I've just received a message from the hospital," Craig imparted quickly. "Father Silvas is feeling a bit better and he would like to see you in your wedding dress."

Velana's eyes lit up. "Well, let's get over there with the whole shebang." Rounding up her bridesmaids she instructed them to fall in behind her as Craig took her arm and led her out of the marquee and across the road to the hospital, followed by their entourage in all their regalia.

Father Silvas was sitting up in bed, propped against the pillows, the only sign that there was anything wrong with him showing in a slight twisting of his mouth. But his eyes still shone with the sparkle of life and they lit up at the sight of the bridal party parading in through the ward to visit him.

Velana knelt down beside him, kissed his hand, and made the sign of the cross.

"God bless you, my child," he murmured. "You look wonderful, I'm so glad you came." Taking Craig's hand he congratulated him and said, "Open that bedside drawer, you'll find a wedding gift for you both."

Craig opened the drawer and took out a little parcel, so carefully wrapped, and handed it to Velana. She undid the bow and it fell open and to her amazement it was a little 'still' made of pure gold. The inscription read *'To Velana and Craig, two wonderful people who have blessed our village with love and happiness'*.

"Open the lid," Father Silvas directed. Velana lifted the top portion of the ornament and a tinkling musical sound filled the air. It was one of Velana's songs 'Que Deus Me Perdoe'.

A silent hush wafted through the ward as Velana began to sing the melody, to the accompaniment of the music from the still. The doctors and nurses stopped what they were doing to listen, enchanted by the beautiful sound of Velana's voice, and when she finally finished singing there was hardly a dry eye in the ward.

Father Silvas gave a sigh and said, "That was wonderful, Velana, so haunting and yet so full of charm." He took a hand each of Velana and Craig and whispered.

"Now go into the future and travel through the poppy field of life together. God bless you both."

Velana felt too choked up to say goodbye, and she went away quickly, turning to give the old priest a little wave as she left the ward.

They all returned to the marquee. The party was still going full swing. Collette and Iona were jubilant, and they assured Velana that her wedding day had been a triumph from beginning to end.

"All weddings should be like this," cried Collette, trying to be heard above the sound of the band and the party guests enjoying themselves.

During one of the quieter moments of the celebrations, Iona produced two beautiful framed pictures and handed them to Velana, smiling as she said, "These are our wedding present to you. Collette painted one and I painted the other."

Velana gasped and showed them to Craig – two watercolours of Corrish, both capturing the mystical atmosphere of the island, the dense woodland in the high valley, the loch in the mid-distance, and the moisture-laden clouds mantling the triple peaks in the far distance.

"They're beautiful." Velana was overcome. "But how did you know that's where we're going on our honeymoon?"

"It was only a guess, but we thought you might," laughed Collette. "And don't worry about the twins, we'll help Theresa to look after them and make sure they go to school and church and do their homework."

Craig brushed his lips across Velana's neck and whispered in her ear, "It's time, my love, it's time for us to go. We had better get changed."

Velana hugged Iona and Collette in turn, then she

beckoned Theresa, Guida, and Maria, to come and help her to get dressed. She had chosen a lilac linen suit for her going-away outfit, with matching shoes and handbag.

"You look lovely, Mrs Ferguson," said Theresa as she put some finishing touches to Velana's hair. Tears of happiness filled the eyes of mother and daughter. "*Eu Te Adoro*, Mamma," whispered Velana. Taking the little coloured carved candle from the centre of her bouquet she rolled it up in tissue and placed it carefully in her handbag. "I shall cherish this and keep it forever, then I shall always be reminded of this perfect day."

Theresa embraced her lovingly. "Craig is waiting for you, sweetheart. Go to your husband and have a wonderful honeymoon."

Velana rejoined the rest of the wedding party, Theresa, Maria and Guida, still fussing with her dress and hair, wanting her to look her best for Craig who was standing patiently waiting for her to appear.

"Thank you, thank you all," Velana said with tears in her eyes. "As always, I could never have done any of it without you."

Craig took his bride by the hand and led her through the corridor of rejoicing guests, to their waiting car. For a brief moment, Velana held her bouquet high above her head, then she threw it into the happy crowd, neatly caught by Guida to the roars and cheers of the others.

As Craig and Velana sped into the clear moonlit evening, she gave a final wave to her friends and relations. Theresa, her loving Mamma, who had always given her guidance and love; Guida and Collette, her special friends and mentors; Maria; Farmer Rodrigas; Pedro; her three half-sisters – Iona, Heather, and Kirsty – brought to her by a wonderful trick of fate . . . and Edward, Eva, and Craig. Her family was complete . . .

Except – how wonderful if Ian had been here, and Papa Mario and Miguel too . . . but it was not to be; they were part of the past now – part of a pattern that had been rich and fulfilling.

She paused for a moment, remembering Jose. It had all begun with him really, the love, the magic, the caring . . . he would always have a special place in her heart.

She put her head against Craig's shoulder as they drove away from the little market town. The church bells were ringing out for evening service and Velana remembered the words of Father Silvas. *"Go into the future and travel through the poppy field of life together, and God bless you both."*